"Only one thing will fix all this. If you marry me..."

It took a few seconds for his words to sink in. "Marry you? You can't be serious." But Anita could see that he was. "Why would you even consider marrying me?"

"Let's face it, Anita. You and I have been fighting this attraction between us." Tate's complexion became a bit ruddier. "I didn't mean that the way it sounded. Look, spending time around you and your kids has made me realize what I've been missing. I think marrying you would be the right move for me. You'd gain the financial security you need and I'd get a ready-made family."

Anita didn't care about Tate's money. The only reason she would consider marriage to him was her deepening feelings for him.

He would be the rescuer and protector, but she would be the one in love....

Dear Reader,

April is an exciting month for the romance industry because that is when our authors learn whether or not their titles have been nominated for the prestigious RITA® Award sponsored by the Romance Writers of America. As with the Oscars, our authors will find out whether they've actually won in a glamorous evening event that caps off the RWA national conference in July. Of course, all the Silhouette Romance titles this month are already winners to me!

Karen Rose Smith heads up this month's lineup with her tender romance *To Protect and Cherish* (#1810) in which a cowboy-at-heart bachelor becomes a father overnight. *Prince Incognito* (#1811) by Linda Goodnight features another equally unforgettable hero—this one a prince masquerading as an ordinary guy. Nearly everyone accepts his disguise except, of course, our perceptive heroine who is now torn between the dictates of her head…and her heart. Longtime Silhouette Romance author Sharon De Vita returns with *Doctor's Orders* (#1812), in which a single mother who has been badly burned by love discovers a handsome doctor just might have the perfect prescription for her health and longtime happiness. Finally, in Roxann Delaney's *His Queen of Hearts* (#1813), a runaway bride goes from the heat and into the fire when she finds herself holed up in a remote location with her handsome rescuer.

Happy reading!
Sincerely,

Ann Leslie Tuttle
Associate Senior Editor

Please address questions and book requests to:
Silhouette Reader Service
U.S.: 3010 Walden Ave., P.O. Box 1325, Buffalo, NY 14269
Canadian: P.O. Box 609, Fort Erie, Ont. L2A 5X3

KAREN ROSE SMITH

To Protect and Cherish

SILHOUETTE Romance®

Published by Silhouette Books

America's Publisher of Contemporary Romance

With thanks to Stella Bagwell for her Texas expertise and her willingness to answer my questions.

 SILHOUETTE BOOKS

ISBN 0-373-19810-8

TO PROTECT AND CHERISH

Visit Silhouette Books at www.eHarlequin.com

Printed in U.S.A.

KAREN ROSE SMITH,

award-winning author of over fifty published novels, loves to write. She began putting pen to paper in high school but never suspected crafting emotional and romantic stories would become her life's work! Married for thirty-four years, she and her husband reside in Pennsylvania with their two cats, Ebbie and London. Readers can e-mail Karen through her Web site at www.karenrosesmith.com or write to her at P.O. Box 1545, Hanover, PA 17331.

Dear Reader,

The idea for *To Protect and Cherish* came easily. I keep folders of pictures of heroes, heroines and children who might appear in my story lines. In my collection I spotted a magazine photo of a red-headed boy with a devilish grin, holding a frog. I asked myself—What if there were *two* of him? What if the heroine had *more* than two children? What if suddenly the hero took on responsibility for a family and had to learn to become a dad overnight?

I love writing about cowboys, men who have an innate sense of integrity, men who protect and cherish those they love. My hero, Tate Pardell, is a cowboy at heart, and I never knew exactly what he was going to say or do next! That's the type of character who makes writing challenging and fun.

I hope you enjoy Tate and the family he vows to protect and cherish.

Karen Rose Smith

Chapter One

"You have three kids?"

Tate Pardell ran his hand through his thick, dark-brown hair and took a second look at the young woman who sat across from his desk. When she'd walked into his office at Pardell Construction, his first look had been long and appreciative. She wasn't beautiful, but with those green eyes, auburn curls and an abundance of freckles—never mind the delicious curves—his reaction hadn't been an appropriate one, considering she was interviewing for the position of housekeeper.

As Anita Sutton's cheeks reddened, her chin lifted. "I know you advertised for a housekeeper, never expecting a...a family. But I really need this job, Mr. Pardell. And my kids, well—"

"I need a housekeeper, but I was looking for someone older, with no attachments. Like my last one."

"Why did she leave?" Anita asked.

Tate leaned back in the mahogany captain's chair, studying Anita carefully. He had intended to do the interviewing, but she had turned the tables on him. He decided that was okay for the moment.

"Dorothy turned sixty-five last year, and when I moved into a new house, she said it was too big for her to handle. She decided to retire and went to live with her sister in Waco."

Disconcerted by the eagerness in Anita's green eyes, he read her résumé again. "You don't have any experience as a housekeeper."

"I'm a mother, Mr. Pardell, so I'm a housekeeper every day of my life. As you can see from my résumé, I've waitressed for years. But I'm also self-taught on computers. A while back, I took a course on Web design and started a business. I have a few clients and hope to get more. I want to grow my business so I don't have to waitress *or* be a housekeeper."

"So this job would be only temporary?"

Dressed in black slacks and a cream oxford shirt, Anita fiddled with the button-down collar now, as if she were nervous…as if what he decided mattered a lot. "I'm sure it will take at least a year until my Web design business can support us. You said you need someone now, and here I am."

Yes. Here she was.

Every time he looked at her face, his blood moved a little faster—maybe a lot faster. His gaze rested on a group photo of his employees rather than on her and he was reminded of the reason he'd advertised for a housekeeper. He threw an annual barbecue for his staff. It was a tradition. He needed a housekeeper who could put it together in the next couple of weeks and not be dismayed by the prospect. He needed a woman who could make his house run smoothly so he didn't have to think about it. A woman who would prepare meals and stow them away, so when he came home late he'd have more to eat than beef jerky.

"How old are your kids?" he asked warily. He'd never had any experience with children, and he wasn't sure he wanted it now.

The sweetest smile he'd ever seen spread across Anita's lips. "My twins, Corey and Jared, are five. Little Marie is ten-and-a-half months old."

The surprises kept coming. "You have a baby?"

"She's a very good baby, Mr. Pardell. A sound sleeper. I can't promise you won't know we're around, but I'm a good mother. I don't let the boys run wild, and I keep Marie close."

Picturing this woman as a mother unsettled Tate terribly. Maybe it was because of the stirring he felt when he looked at her. Or maybe it was because his desire and the pictures that came with it didn't go hand in hand with the tableau of a woman caring for children.

"Do you have anyone else who's interviewed for this position?" Anita asked.

Hell, yes, he'd had other women interview for the position! None that he wanted to consider, though. They either didn't do windows, didn't cook or didn't like being stuck out of town on a ranch. There had been one who had sashayed in with long, red fingernails and bleached-blond hair with a look in her eye that told him being Mrs. Tate Pardell was high on her priority list.

In eastern Texas, Pardell Construction was a name that had become well known over the past few years. Tate was proud of his accomplishments and most of the decisions he'd made that had brought him to the place where he was now—respected in the community and financially secure. And more than one woman had seen him as a prize. He'd misjudged the last one and had gotten badly burned. With her innocent vulnerable demeanor, Anita Sutton didn't look as if she had a deceptive bone in her body, but he wasn't so easily fooled now.

"I've interviewed a few other applicants," he finally answered tactfully.

"Let me show you what I can do," Anita responded with some excitement in her voice, sliding to the edge of her chair.

"Show me?"

"Yes. Let me come to your house this weekend and cook a meal for you. Hire me temporarily if you must, until I can prove to you that this can work."

Deciding to see how honest she could be, he asked, "So what's the reason you want this job so badly?" He tried to keep his voice conversationally even, but he wanted the truth. He was going to see if she would give it.

When Anita looked down at her hands, her curly, shoulder-length hair hid her face. Then she raised her gaze to his once more. "When my husband died a year ago, I vowed to my kids I'd provide them with a good life. I don't want to just take care of their basic needs— I want to send them to college. That's why I took that adult-ed class on Web design. But Larry left bills. I have to pay medical expenses for the week after the accident…the week before he died. In addition, I had more medical bills when Marie was born. I'm not covering our expenses as a waitress, and last month my rent went up again. I need something steady that pays more until my business gets off the ground. The salary you offered is generous, and the room and board would be a godsend. I could save a lot of my salary, pay off debts and then build a small nest egg."

He knew what she was saying could be true. However, before he sampled her cooking, before he tested her as a housekeeper, he had to know more about those kids. He just couldn't imagine three of them underfoot. Then again, he wasn't home that much.

"Are your boys in school yet?"

"They start Tuesday. All day in kindergarten."

As he checked his watch, he asked, "So they're home now?"

"I have a neighbor who babysits for me. She comes to my apartment."

Making a decision, he stood. "All right, I want to meet them."

When he came around the desk, he saw her eyes start at his boots and run up his six-foot-two frame. It made him hot, thinking she was checking him out in the same way that he'd appraised her.

"Now?" she asked, her voice high and unsure.

He wanted to catch the kids unawares. He wanted to see her place. He wanted to find out what kind of woman she was before he seriously considered employing her and let her into his house. "Yes, now. Is that a problem?"

When she rose, too, she seemed like such a little bit of a thing. Maybe five-foot-four? "No…No problem. Uh, do you want my address?"

"I'll follow you." When she looked troubled, he asked, "What's wrong? Is there a reason you *don't* want me to go home with you now?" He wondered if she'd been lying about something and he was going to catch her in it.

Blushing again, she admitted, "It's just that my apartment might not be straightened up."

"Might not?"

She gave a nervous little laugh. "Well, with kids…" She stopped, not wanting to sink her chances of getting the job.

"Yes? With kids?"

"Never mind," she said, turning toward the door. "Let's go." Without another look at him, she pushed open the glass door to Pardell Construction and went outside into the bright August day.

Tate followed her, wondering just what in the heck he was getting himself into.

As Anita cast a glance at Tate Pardell following her in his red SUV, she was a nervous wreck. She *did* need this job. Desperately. Her debts included the charges Larry had racked up on their credit card before he died. She didn't know how she was going to do it, but she wanted to pay back the people they owed.

When she snuck a peek at Tate again and caught the intent expression under his tan Stetson as he drove, her pulse raced. She'd never expected to be attracted to him. She'd scoped him out on the Internet before calling because she wouldn't move her kids into just anyone's house. Not that she could tell character from a few newspaper articles, but she'd learned enough to make her set up the interview. He had money, that was true. He'd dated lots of women—model types—that was also true. However, he was involved in charitable work. There had been a picture of him serving soup at a shelter for the homeless. He apparently helped out every weekend during the winter months. A man who did that on his free time had to have some place in his heart that was filled with goodness. At least enough goodness that she and her kids would be safe in his house.

Meeting him had reinforced her opinion.

Truth be told, she didn't expect much of men anymore. Her father had disappeared before she was born and Larry had certainly let her down. But she wouldn't be involved in Tate Pardell's personal life; she'd be his employee—his housekeeper—and that was all she cared about.

On Friday afternoons, curbside parking in front of her apartment was available. Her unit was one of eight in a two-story building. It wasn't in the best part of town, but she had good neighbors. She'd hung a dried-flower wreath on the door and planted marigolds in a window box decorating the single window. After she pulled to a stop, she heard the purr of Tate's engine behind her as he parked. Climbing out of her car, she led the way to her doorstep.

When Tate met her there, he muttered, "I hope you don't go out alone at night." He glanced at the abandoned building next to the apartment, then across the street, where the row houses were run-down.

Her shoulders squared. "Clear Springs is too small to have a high crime rate."

"No place is immune from drugs and guns these days," he returned.

"If I could move us into a better area, I would," she said defensively.

With one booted foot on the first step, his hand in one pocket, his Stetson drawn low, he gave her a penetrating look. Then he responded, "Yes, I suppose you would." He motioned in front of him. "Lead the way."

The August afternoon was almost balmy, and a breeze lifted a few curls along her cheek. As she passed Tate, his forearm brushed her wrist and she felt the contact in too many places. Covering her sudden awareness of him, she found her house key on the ring and unlocked the door.

When she stepped inside the living room, she breathed a sigh of relief. Coloring books and crayons littered the scarred coffee table, and two pairs of small sneakers lay in front of the TV. Other than that, the room was clean and neat.

Tate was looking around with interest, and Anita tried to see her place through his eyes. She'd made the ruffled yellow-and-blue plaid curtains on the windows with her neighbor's sewing machine. The slipcover on the sofa matched. Red throw pillows on the couch were the same material as the covering on her platform rocker. Purple, yellow and white snapdragons from the backyard stood in a mason jar on the pine table by the side of the chair, while photos of Corey, Jared and Marie peered out from discount-store frames on a small set of bookshelves.

Framed finger paintings the twins had created hung above the sofa. She loved the coziness of her living room, but as Tate Pardell scanned it, she realized he probably thought it looked like bargain store chic.

Suddenly, something occurred to her and she spun around to face him. "Would you even have room for me and three kids?"

He looked uncomfortable, as if he didn't want to say if he would or wouldn't. But then he answered her. "There'd be room. The house has quarters for a maid or housekeeper—two bedrooms, a sitting room and a full bath. You'd have to use the main kitchen, but otherwise, it's about as much room as you have here."

She couldn't keep the surprise from her voice. "Your house must be huge!"

He gave a short laugh. "That's one of the terms Dorothy used."

"Do you have a lot of family?"

"I didn't build the house for family," he answered tersely and left it at that.

Maybe he'd built it as a status symbol. Or maybe it wasn't as big as she was imagining.

Laughter and chatter were coming from the kitchen, and she motioned toward it. "As you can hear, everyone's in there." Taking a deep breath, Anita decided she might as well get this over with. If he didn't like little boys, they were sunk, because Corey and Jared were *all* boy.

As soon as Anita stepped into the kitchen, she could have groaned. Of all the days for the boys to be finger painting with chocolate pudding.

Over at the sink, Inez Jamison was washing dishes

in soapy water. She was almost sixty and wore her gray hair in a thick braid that dangled between her shoulder blades. She was plump, and as she turned, her round face wore a smile. When she spied Tate, the smile faded as her brown eyes sped to Anita for an explanation.

Corey and Jared, oblivious to the adults, were happily smearing pudding on each other's papers. They had the dessert in their red hair and in between freckles on their faces. It looked as if they'd been eating more of it than painting with it. They were loud and laughing, and Anita was afraid she'd already lost the housekeeping position.

"Boys," she called clearly in a firm tone above the ruckus.

After sloshing his pudding-covered hand over Jared's paper, Corey looked up at her.

Jared elbowed his brother, giggled and then gave his mother his attention. "Hey, Mom, you're home. Look what we're doin'."

In spite of herself and the situation, Anita had to smile. Going over to her boys, she found a spot on each of their cheeks that wasn't sticky and kissed them.

As they'd been doing lately, they both shied away.

"Aw, Mom," Jared complained, "don't get mushy."

When she heard a chuckle come from Tate, she thought that might be a good sign. "I'm going to be mushy until you're eighteen, then I'll *think* about not being mushy. I want you to meet somebody."

Now both boys stared at Tate.

"Mr. Pardell, these are my sons, Corey and Jared." She laid a hand on each of their heads as she said their names. "And this is Inez Jamison. She's my neighbor and good friend."

Tate tipped his Stetson. "It's good to meet you all."

"And just who are you?" Inez asked, drying her hands on a towel. Inez was always point-blank forward and said what she thought.

Tate took off his Stetson and held it in one hand. "I run a construction company."

"You're thinking about constructing something here?" Inez asked, eyebrows raised.

At that, Tate chuckled again. "Not exactly. I'm interviewing Mrs. Sutton for a job."

"Corey, Jared," Anita said again, taking their attention from smearing goop on each other. "Why don't you go wash up?"

"Aw, Mom." The wail came from Jared.

"If you wash up now without complaining, I might let you go outside and play baseball."

"Beat you to the bathroom," Corey said to his brother, and like lightning, was off the chair and down the hall. Jared ran after him.

"They sure can move fast when there's something they want to do. I'd better make sure you don't end up with pudding on your shower curtain," Inez commented, looking after them.

"They're a little rowdy at times, but they're good boys," she told Tate. "And you won't find a better mother anywhere. Marie's a little angel, and if you can't appreciate that—"

Gently, Anita draped her arm around Inez's shoulders. "I can handle it from here. Marie's napping?"

"Been down about an hour. She'll be waking up soon. It might take a little while to wash up the boys. I think they both got pudding on their shirts. I'll find them clean ones."

After Inez left the kitchen, Anita looked around at the small space that appeared as if a tornado had hit it. The Formica table, as well as the construction paper, was smeared with chocolate pudding. Finished paintings lay drying on the counter, while an overturned dump truck blocked the back door. One of the boys' baseball caps had fallen from its peg on the wall.

Suddenly, Jared was back in the kitchen, still sticky.

"You're not washed up yet," Anita noted.

"Corey's going first. I had a question for Mr. Pardell."

Uh-oh. Anita never knew what was going to come out of Jared's mouth.

"I want to know if I can try on your hat."

Embarrassed, Anita grabbed Jared's hand right before he got chocolate pudding on Tate's hat. "Whoa. Mr. Pardell doesn't want to buy a new Stetson. It's really not polite to ask if you can try on someone else's clothes."

"Why not?" Jared wanted to know.

His whys somehow had her thinking up very creative answers. This time, she said simply, "Clothes are personal and private. Remember, we've talked about private?"

"Just like we talked about strangers and not going anywhere with them. Are you a stranger?" he asked Tate.

Crouching down, Tate looked the boy in the eye. "Yes, I'm a stranger now. But if we get to know one another better, then we won't be strangers."

"You mean like playing ball together or somethin'?"

"Playing ball more than one time. And only if your mom approved."

The five-year-old seemed to think that over. "How long does it take until you're not a stranger anymore?"

Tate glanced up at Anita, then back at her son. "That's a very good question and I'm not sure." He pointed to Jared's chest and tapped it. "You have to know in there that the other person likes you, won't hurt you and isn't going to be gone so fast you'll never see him again."

Cocking his head, Jared mulled it over, then asked, "You mean like a man coming to the door selling something?"

"Exactly." Tate stood once more.

"So if we was friends, I could try on your Stetson?"

Anita could see Tate was trying to suppress a grin. "If we were friends, I think I'd let you try on my Stetson." He looked down at the little boy's hands. "*If* your hands were clean."

"Are you going to be our friend?"

Anita had had enough. If Jared's questions hadn't made Tate turn tail and run yet, they soon would. She nudged her son toward the bathroom. "Go wash up now. If that pudding dries too much, you won't be able to get it off."

"I'll have to go to school like this," he said gleefully.

Shaking her head, Anita practically walked her son to the bathroom, then came back to face Tate.

"I'm sorry about all that," Anita began. "Five-year-olds are full of questions. But we'd respect your privacy." Whether he believed her or not, Anita couldn't tell.

Tate nodded to the hall. "Your daughter's sleeping?"

"Yes. But we can peek in. Like I said, she's a sound sleeper." Maybe if she could convince him of that it would help.

* * *

When Tate walked into Anita's bedroom, he felt an increase in the turmoil he'd begun to experience standing in her kitchen. His family had broken apart, piece by piece, when he was a kid, and he'd felt responsible. He'd felt as if he were to blame for his brother's death. Because they'd lost Jeremy, his parents had gotten divorced, so he'd always carried the burden of that, too. In his adult life, he'd worked, bedded women and worked some more, telling himself he was happy with his freedom…happy being responsible only for himself. Yet, as he'd stepped into Anita Sutton's kitchen, seen firsthand the bond between her and her boys and the neighbor who helped her out, he'd remembered what it felt like to be part of a family. An old yearning had kicked him in the gut and was still doing it.

On top of that, he now realized the baby didn't have her own bedroom. Her crib was situated beside Anita's bed. The living room had smelled like cinnamon. In this room, he caught a whiff of vanilla, and then he saw the potpourri dish on the dresser. There was an inexpensive perfume bottle there, and a small wooden chest. The coverlet on the bed was pale-blue, which he figured must be Anita's favorite color since it was prominent in the living room, too. When his gaze veered to the bed, he was bombarded by images of himself holding Anita in it. That was absolutely insane! He didn't even know the woman. And he certainly didn't want his life disrupted by three kids in his house, did he?

As he followed Anita to the other side of the bed, he saw the little girl in the crib. There was such an odd feeling in his chest that he didn't know what to make of it. Inez Jamison had called her an "angel," and she certainly looked like one. Her strawberry-blond hair curled in ringlets as she lay on her side, sucking her thumb. Dressed in a yellow terry cloth playsuit, she was absolutely oblivious to them. He caught the whiff of a sweet, clean smell as he stepped closer to the crib.

"She's beautiful," he murmured, his throat constricting a little.

"I think so, too," Anita said softly.

Still looking down at the baby, he asked, "She was born after your husband died?"

"Six weeks after."

He could only imagine how hard that must have been for Anita, to go through labor and delivery all alone. He was getting the feeling that she was a strong woman.

"How did your husband die?" he asked, keeping his voice low.

There was a momentary hesitation before Anita responded. "He was a flagman on a road construction crew. He was handling traffic on a curve at dusk. It had started raining and another crew member said he stepped out into the lane of traffic for something. The driver didn't see him because Larry had taken off his vest."

Tate's gaze met hers. "I'm sorry." He was sorry for her on more than one account. If the driver had been at fault, she would have received an insurance settlement. As it was, the blame had been with her deceased husband.

"He didn't have life insurance?"

"The company provided a small policy, but it just paid for the funeral expenses."

They were both beside the crib now, standing very close. Tate wanted to reach out and finger one of Anita's curls. He wanted to run his thumb over those freckles and kiss her pretty lips.

What was *wrong* with him? They were standing here, talking about her deceased husband, and he wanted to kiss her!

Yet, he could see there was an awareness of him as a man in her eyes, as well as questions, curiosity and hope. It was the hope that got to him.

He said gruffly, "We'd better go back to the living room to talk." Then he broke eye contact and strode away from the crib and Anita.

If he knew what was good for him, he wouldn't even consider her for the housekeeper position. He didn't want his life turned upside down. He certainly didn't want to hear the pitter-patter of footsteps around the house, did he?

The pitter-patter of footsteps. Children's laughter. Questions only five-year-olds could come up with.

Anita had followed him to the living room and now gently touched his elbow. He felt that touch through his denim sleeve, all the way to—

"Mr. Pardell, don't make a decision right now. Let me cook that meal for you."

"You want to convince me through my stomach?" he asked with an arched brow.

"If I have to."

Suddenly he wondered what else she'd do to get the job. Was she like Donna? Did she believe once she finagled her way into his life she could use him to make herself secure? To give herself position in the community? To buy her every heart's desire?

Her green eyes seemed so sincere. He knew she really *did* need this job. "You want to cook with or without your kids underfoot?"

"Inez might be able to watch them tomorrow, if that's what you have in mind."

"Do you pay her to watch them?"

"We use the bartering system. She never learned to drive, so I run errands for her and do her grocery shopping."

"What did she do before you became her neighbor?"

"She would make more than one trip from the corner grocery. Everything was more expensive there, so I save her money by shopping for her at the discount store, too."

"I see. And what would happen if you *do* get this job?"

"I could still run errands for her and shop for groceries on my day off. I *would* have a day off, wouldn't I?"

"Of course. Sunday and one other day of the week you pick. I'm not a slave driver."

"That's good to know," she said agreeably.

She was walking him down a flowered lane, making him imagine her in his house, her food in his stomach. She wasn't only strong; she was smart, too.

"All right. If you want to cook a meal for me, cook a meal. I'll set it up with the manager at Blake's Market over on Kingston. Buy whatever you need and he'll put it on my tab. What time do you think you'll have to start?"

"What would you like me to make? What's your favorite meal?"

"I don't have a favorite."

"Do you watch your diet?"

"If you mean, am I a health nut? No. Though I do eat chicken once in a while instead of beef."

"How about fried chicken, mashed potatoes, fresh green beans and an apple pie?"

She *really* wanted this job, and he knew he was going to regret this, but he said, "That sounds fine."

"Great. Then I'll be over about three in the afternoon and we'll plan supper for six. Will you be home?"

"I'll be there. I'm having two horses delivered tomorrow."

"I'll need directions."

"Go south on Longhorn, five miles past the traffic light. Turn left onto Pine Grove Road. After a mile, you'll see a lane on the right. My mailbox is there at the end of the lane."

She extended her hand to him. "Thanks for giving me this chance."

After he took her hand, he was sorry he did because it was small, feminine and warm. Just like her. A shot of electricity jolted him at the touch of her skin, and after a quick shake, he pulled away.

"Tomorrow at three," he said, heading for the door.

"See you tomorrow," he heard as he stepped out onto the small porch and charged down the steps.

He would not think about Anita Sutton again until tomorrow. If she somehow crept into his thoughts, he'd just imagine chocolate pudding smeared on his new oak kitchen set.

That ought to keep everything in perspective.

Chapter Two

As Anita drove up the long lane to Tate Pardell's house the next afternoon, she was impressed. The split-rail fencing seemed to go on forever. The brick-and-tan-siding ranch house sprawled across the land, and she fleetingly wondered how much acreage belonged with it. Anita had only caught a glimpse of a tall white barn behind the house, but she guessed there were other out-buildings, too.

Gathering up the grocery bags, she went to the front door and rang the bell. Instead of a chime, the Yellow Rose of Texas played and she smiled.

A few seconds later, Tate opened the door, dressed in jeans and a light blue, snap-button shirt with the sleeves rolled back over his forearms. His thick brown hair had an unruly wave. As a lock of it fell over his forehead, her fingers itched to brush it back, and she realized the chemistry was starting again. Why did she feel like this when she got within ten feet of him?

Without giving her a chance to take a breath, he gathered the bags into his arms, saying, "I'll carry those."

"Really, it's—"

As he took the bags from her, one of his hands touched her waist, his other her breast. Their gazes locked and she felt the entire world stand still.

Then he was turning away, carrying the groceries inside.

Stepping into the foyer, she closed the door, still burning from the heat of his touch, still shaken by the chemistry between them. Unless it was all one-sided. She could pray it was all one-sided…all on her part.

Over his shoulder, he said, "I just got a call. The horses will be arriving any minute."

She was in awe of her surroundings. This house must have cost a small fortune! To the right she saw the great room with a cathedral ceiling, fan and skylights. There was a dining room to its left, where a hand-carved oak table and chairs could easily seat eight. She could almost see into the kitchen, and she realized there were many more rooms. What surrounded her now was the center of the house. Why did one man need all this space? It was obvious from the look and feel of the rooms that he wasn't here very much. This could have been a model home open to the public.

The kitchen was as impressive as the rest of the house, with its smooth range top, side-by-side refrigerator that had beautiful oak doors to match the cupboards, and ceramic-tiled floor in shades of blue, cream and rust. A smaller, round oak table sat under an antler chandelier.

"Your house is beautiful," she commented as she went to the bags on the table.

When he set the sack of apples on the counter, a few of them tumbled out. "I built it myself," he said proudly, then amended, "Well, one of my construction crews did."

"And you live here alone?" She didn't know any other way to tactfully ask if he might have a live-in significant other.

"Yes, I live here alone."

Taking the chicken she'd bought, she quickly stowed it away in the refrigerator. Then she did the same with the eggs, avoiding his gaze and curbing her own curiosity.

He motioned to the remaining bags on the table. "This looks as if you're going to feed an army."

"I'm planning for you to have leftovers. You might not have to eat out all week. You'll have to show me where everything is. I brought a pie plate and a pastry cloth in case you don't have them, but I'll need a large skillet and a vegetable steamer."

With a quick motion, he opened two bottom cupboards. "I bought a full set of cookware and haven't touched it, except for the small frying pan. In a way, you're going to be christening the kitchen today and giving it its first full workout."

Taking a pastry cloth from her bag, she spread it on the counter.

"What's that?"

"That's where I'll roll the dough for the piecrust."

"Are you sure you shouldn't be opening a restaurant instead of going into Web design?"

She vigorously shook her head. "Cooking's a hobby. It won't take me where I want to go."

"Where is that?"

He looked interested, and rarely did she have a chance to share her hopes. When she'd been married to Larry, everything had always been about *his* dreams. Pipe dreams. Dreams that never had any substance.

The words tumbled from her mouth. "I want a better life. Eventually I want to become a graphic designer."

"I moved out *here* to this ranch to create a better life," he mused. "I want to run some cattle and train a few horses."

"You come from a ranching background?"

"I lived on a ranch until my parents divorced. They raised Herefords. When my father sold the spread and moved to Arizona, I missed it."

"You didn't go with him?"

"No. I stayed here with my mother until I went to college. After the University of Texas, I apprenticed, got my contractor's license and started Pardell Construction."

"Do you see your dad much?"

"No. I call him or he calls me about every six months."

"Is your mom still here?"

"No. She's living in Taos now. She went there to find herself."

"Has she? Found herself?"

His smile was crooked. "As much as she's going to."

Suspecting that there was a lot more story behind Tate's simple words, Anita found herself interested in knowing what that story was. There was a lot he wasn't saying. Her own background had led her to make the choices that she had—wrong choices. Apparently, Tate's background had led him to make the right ones.

"It sounds as if you've always known what you wanted."

He treated her comment lightly. "Not exactly. I had rodeo aspirations when I was a teenager. I thought bull riding was going to be my ticket to fame and fortune. But then I got some sense. I still try it every now and then, though, to make sure I haven't lost the knack."

Anita shook her head. "Men never grow up."

Taking a step closer to her…so close she caught the scent of sun and hard work…so close she saw the faint scar on his left cheek…so close she could count the springy brown hairs curling between the plackets of his open shirt collar…he warned her, "Don't lump us all together."

Swallowing hard, she would have taken a step back, but she couldn't because the counter was behind her. "You could get hurt riding bulls."

His blue eyes studied her and seemed to settle on her lips. "I could get hurt doing a lot less."

There was an edge to his voice that made her wonder exactly why he still *did* ride bulls. "Why go looking for trouble?"

When he seemed to lean a little nearer, she found herself focusing on his lips and what they'd feel like on hers.

"Sometimes trouble comes knocking whether you want it or not," Tate philosophized.

Was he talking about her? Taking on her and her kids in his house? Was he still against the idea? She knew Tate

Pardell could be trouble to *her* with a capital *T.* He was too handsome, too appealing, too sexy, too…everything.

"You said men never grow up. Was that true of your husband?" he asked.

With Tate so close she couldn't think straight. "Mr. Pardell—"

"It's Tate," he reminded her gruffly.

"Tate, I don't think we should discuss my marriage."

"Why not? If I give you this job we should know something about each other."

"If you give me this job? Are you considering it?"

"I'm considering it." The light in his eyes said he was considering other things, too. Just as she was.

Suddenly, two long blares of a horn sounded outside. She blinked.

Tate moved away.

"That would be the horses," he said, straightening. "Are you going to be all right in here?"

Yes, she'd be perfectly fine once he left the kitchen. She'd be perfectly fine once she knew she could pay her bills for this month. She'd be perfectly fine once she figured out how to give her children a future.

"I'm sure I can find everything I need in here," she responded nonchalantly, though she wasn't feeling nonchalant at all.

With a nod, he walked to the hat caddy by the back door, took his Stetson from it and fixed it on his head. Then he left the kitchen and closed the door, the sound reverberating in Anita's ears.

She knew better than to get involved with *any* man. The only thing *that* would bring would be disappointment. Her marriage had been one disappointment after another, one lonely night after another, one worry after another. Her children were her focus, and she just needed to put a good, solid roof over their heads. She just needed a reprieve from bills that wouldn't quit. This job could be the solution to so many problems.

And Tate Pardell?

He was the solution to none. She vowed to remember that as she cooked him a meal he'd never forget.

As Anita worked, she remembered the days after Larry's funeral and the itemized credit card bills she'd examined more closely than she had before. Devastatingly, those bills had proved her husband had had an affair, maybe more than one. She'd asked herself why she hadn't seen his deception sooner. The answer had been easy—she hadn't *wanted* to see. She'd wanted the fairy tale, although her life had been far from it. She'd wanted a man to believe in. Larry hadn't been that man. She didn't know if any man could be that man because she wasn't sure she'd ever trust one again.

While Anita rolled out pie dough, she glanced out the kitchen window often and watched Tate help unload the horses. One was black with four white stockings. The other was pewter gray. As he backed them down the ramps, he seemed gentle with them. When he leaned toward their ears, she wondered if he was crooning to them in that way some trainers did—the trainers who didn't believe in breaking horses but rather gentling them.

As Tate and the driver of the truck disappeared into the barn, she slid the pie dough shell onto the plate,

rolled out the second, then sliced apples, mixed them
with cinnamon, brown sugar, flour and butter and loaded
up the pie dish. An hour later, the pie was golden-brown,
sending its sweet, cinnamony scent throughout the
kitchen. The driver of the horse trailer had left, but Tate
was still inside the barn. Humming a favorite country-
western tune by LeAnn Rimes, Anita peeled potatoes,
called Inez to check on the kids, snapped beans to ready
them for the steamer and began preparing the chicken.

Tate's cupboards were stocked, and the supplies
she'd bought were superfluous. But most of his supplies
had never been opened. He must have gone to the
grocery store because the refrigerator was stocked with
eggs, bacon, cheese, orange juice and a few long-necked
bottles of beer. There was also a slice of pizza that had
definitely sat in there much too long.

Why did he want a house like this if he wasn't going
to spend time in it?

Anita took a stroll into the great room while she
waited for the potatoes to boil. There were no drapes or
even scatter rugs on the hardwood floor. The rough,
plastered white walls were bare, and furniture dotted the
periphery of the room. Not at all the way *she'd* arrange
it. The stone mantel above the beautiful fireplace was
bare and held no pictures or decorative items of any
kind. Fabric on the furniture reminded her of sky and
earth—blue and tan, with a tiny thread of claret running
through the material. She wondered if the rest of the
rooms in the house were so sparsely arranged. Although
she was curious about the housekeeper's quarters, she
wasn't going to go snooping.

* * *

When Tate came in from outside, his nostrils were still full of horses and leather and new-barn smells. Soon, however, the down-home, mouthwatering, tantalizing aromas of the meal Anita had made replaced all of the others. She was removing the golden-brown chicken pieces from the frying pan when he moved closer to her to take a look.

"It smells great!" he said, enthusiastic in spite of himself. All the while he'd gotten the new horses settled, he'd repeated over and over that even though he'd told her he was considering it, no matter how good Anita's cooking was, he *wasn't* going to hire her.

"I'll have it all on the table in two minutes if you want to wash up."

He saw she'd only set one place at the table. "Aren't you going to join me?"

"Oh, no. I have to get home to the kids. Unless you want me to clean up."

His kitchen looked almost as spotless as it had before she'd started cooking. Yet now there was a warmth to it that hadn't been there before. All that remained were the skillet on the stove and the serving dishes on the table.

"I can manage to load the dishwasher myself," he joked.

"I know you can. But if *I* were your housekeeper, you wouldn't have to."

She was pushing, and pushing hard. The care she'd taken with this meal showed that. The truth was, with all this delicious food sitting before him, he had no recourse but to think about coming home to it every night. "Do you cook like this all the time?"

"When I don't have to stretch the budget with macaroni and cheese."

"*Homemade* macaroni and cheese?"

"What other kind is there?" she asked, teasing.

With her face turned up to his, a smile prettying up her lips, her green eyes sparkling, Tate wanted to kiss her more than he wanted to sample the delicious-looking food. He had a feeling kissing Anita would be even more delicious.

Somehow, as they were talking, he'd leaned closer to her and she'd leaned closer to him. Now he straightened and backed away.

"The food's going to get cold if I don't get to it. If you want to get going, go ahead."

His brisk tone made her blink. She was about to pick up the platter when he said, "I'll get that," took it from her and set it on the table.

"Besides cooking…" She stopped herself.

"Yes?"

"Well, it's not my place, but I could make your house more attractive, too."

"What's wrong with the house?"

"You don't have any curtains. Or rugs on the floor. Or pictures on the wall."

"I need those?" he asked wryly.

"Not *need*, exactly. But if you plan to have any guests, you'll want them to feel welcome. The way your great room's arranged, it would be hard to have a conversation."

"I don't get it."

"The armchairs are too far from the sofa. You've got that beautiful fireplace. You could have a grouping around it that would be much cozier."

"You were a decorator in a past life?"

Her cheeks reddened. "No, and I've had no official training. But I do think I have a knack for it."

When he'd wanted furniture for the house, he'd gone into a store, pointed to the pieces he'd liked and that was it. A decorator hadn't seemed necessary. But now he was seeing his house through her eyes. It did have a coldness about it. It certainly didn't have the hominess her living room had, in spite of expensive furniture.

Resting his hands on the back of a chair, he told her the truth. "Anita, I just can't imagine having three kids running around here. That's not my life."

"What *is* your life?"

"I'm a loner. I have been since—since a long time back."

"Do you like being alone?" she asked softly.

That was neither here nor there. "I've gotten used to it. And you know what they say about a man who's set in his ways."

"What do they say?"

"They say it'll drive him nuts to change them."

She looked so disappointed, he felt as if he'd been stabbed. She'd been counting on this job, he could see that.

But she didn't pout or turn bitter and resentful. Rather, she motioned to the rooms behind the kitchen. "Are those the housekeeper's quarters?"

He nodded.

"If it's true you don't spend much time here, you wouldn't even have to see us much. I could cook dinner and take the kids in there in the evenings. They go to bed early anyway. You wouldn't even hear us. I'd make sure the boys didn't leave toys out here for you to trip over. I guess what I'm asking is, please just give it a try. A week, even. Then if it's true that we are in your way and disturb your life, we'll go back to our apartment."

She was making it damn hard for him to refuse. His gaze went again to the food on the table. "Let me think about it. You go on home and I'll give you a call with my decision."

"You promise you'll call and won't just leave me hanging?"

He didn't like the underlying message in that question. It told him men had left her hanging before. Thinking about that disturbed him. "I won't leave you hanging. I'll let you know by Monday at the latest. And whatever I decide won't be temporary. When I make a decision, I stick by it."

"Thank you," she murmured.

The urge to take her in his arms and just hold her and tell her everything was going to be all right was so strong, he had to fight it with every ounce of self-restraint he possessed.

Giving him a smile, she picked up her purse lying on the counter. Cheerily, she advised him, "Make sure you cover everything tightly so it will keep for you. You should have meals for the next few days."

"You don't know my appetite."

Her eyes widened a bit and her lips parted a little in

surprise. They both knew he was talking about more than his liking for fried chicken and mashed potatoes.

Obviously flustered, she broke eye contact, went to the doorway and said, "I'll be waiting to hear from you."

She walked away from his kitchen, into the foyer and out the door. He heard her car start up and the rumble of it scattering gravel as it rolled down his lane. He knew what he *should* do.

Then he took another whiff of the fried chicken and sat down to eat. He'd think about Anita Sutton and her brood *after* he finished the apple pie.

When Tate came calling on Anita Sunday afternoon, her front door was open. Peering through the screen, he didn't hear or see anyone inside. Listening more carefully, he thought he heard boys' laughter out back. That laughter solidified his decision.

Last night, after he'd finished two pieces of apple pie, he'd gone into his great room and looked around. The hollowness of it, the coldness of it, had wrapped around him until he'd been damned uncomfortable. He could get into a rut being alone. He could close himself up, shut everyone out, just as he had after Jeremy died. Just as he had after his parents had gotten divorced. Just as he had after he'd found out Donna's true colors. He might never trust a woman enough to get married—he'd kept the money clip Donna had given him as a reminder to be watchful of women's motives—but that didn't mean he wanted poker night with his buddies to be the main event in his life.

And he did need someone like Anita to plan the barbecue for his employees.

When he tried her screen door, he found it locked. Set on his course now that he'd made a decision, he jogged down the steps and around the apartment building to the backyard. There he saw Anita pitching a ball to one of her twins. He'd have to get straight who was who.

Anita glanced his way about the same time as one of the twins yelled, "Mr. Pardell! Can you pitch a few balls? Mom isn't real good at this."

As Tate laughed, Anita propped her hands on her hips. "Not good at this? Who taught you how to hit home runs?"

Corey piped up, "It's luck when we hit home runs, Mom."

Tate shook his head. "I'll pitch a few," he said with a grin.

"Mr. Pardell, you don't have to…." Anita began.

"It's Tate." His gaze held hers and an electric current that was strong enough to shock him seemed to pass between them.

She didn't repeat his name, though he'd liked to hear it on her lips. Instead, she handed him the ball. "I'm going to check on Marie."

"She's napping?" he asked.

"Yes. I'll be right back. Don't break any windows," she warned with a smile at all three of them.

That smile. Tate kept seeing it in his dreams.

At first, Tate intended to pitch a couple balls and that would be that. He'd offer Anita the job and then go back home to enjoy the rest of the day. But the one or two pitches turned into three, four and five. Instead of just a pitch, he was soon showing Jared how to stand, where to position his bat, how to focus on the ball. Then he did the same for Corey. The twins were eager to listen to him and enthusiastic when it was their turn. Somehow he'd gotten the impression over the years that kids didn't listen. Maybe because at one time *he* hadn't listened? He'd rebelled because he'd missed his brother so badly he hadn't known what to do.

Concentrating on Corey's swing at the ball rather than his own thoughts, Tate heard the click of the door as Anita opened it. She was dressed in jeans today and a Dallas Cowboys T-shirt that had seen many washings. As she held her baby daughter in her arms, Marie laid her head on Anita's shoulder, her thumb in her mouth, her eyes wide and green as she glanced at Tate, then shyly looked away.

As Anita descended the steps, she patted her little girl's back.

Corey and Jared came running over to her. "He's *real* good at baseball," Jared informed her.

"Well, I'm glad. But I don't want you to tire him out. I think you'd better go wash up for supper."

"Oh, Mom," they both complained.

"Mr. Pardell is a busy man, boys. Did you thank him for playing with you?"

In chorus, they said, "Thanks, Mr. Pardell."

"You're most welcome," Tate returned with a grin.

"Go on now, and don't forget to use soap."

This time they didn't argue, but ran up the steps and let the door slam behind them.

Anita shook her head and smiled. "One of these days it's going to come off the hinges." Then realizing what she'd said, she quickly amended, "It's just worn and closes hard. I didn't mean they'd hurt it on purpose."

She was still lobbying for that job, and Tate had to admire her grit. Every time he looked at little Marie, his heart practically turned over. She was such a cute little thing. But he wouldn't be seeing that much of her *or* the boys, he reminded himself.

Getting down to business, he slid his hands into his jeans pockets. "I came over to give you my decision. If you want the job of housekeeper, it's yours. All we can do is see how this works out. If it doesn't, I'll find you something else that pays better than waitressing."

"Oh, thank you, Mr. Pardell. It'll work out just fine," she assured him, beaming.

"Tate," he reminded her.

This time she repeated his name. "Tate."

The sound of it on her lips made his insides jump. She caused way too many physical reactions…way too many erotic thoughts and already a couple of sleepless nights.

"When do you want me to start? I'll have to pack, but we don't have that much. I'll see if I can find a neighbor with a truck—"

"No need for that. Why don't I give you until Wednesday afternoon, when I'll send a couple of crew members and a truck to load everything. We'll have you settled in in no time."

Now she came a little closer to him. "I don't know how to thank you. I know you have your doubts about us moving in, but I'll make it work, and you won't be sorry."

"We'll see about that," he returned gruffly. Then, before he did something stupid like kiss her, before he even had more doubts about the decision he'd made, he repositioned his Stetson on his head. "I'll give you a call and let you know what time for sure on Wednesday."

With a wave of his hand, he left her backyard, trying to erase the picture of her holding her little girl from his mind.

On Tuesday afternoon, the twins were in school when Anita's doorbell buzzed. She'd been packing books from the shelves into cartons. Marie was pulling herself up on the boxes, toddling from one piece of furniture to another and stopping to play with an activity box when she got bored with everything else.

Anita opened the door and found an older couple standing there. The woman, who was a bit plump, wore an expensive-looking blouse and slacks set in a pretty shade of burgundy. Her hair was expertly styled and layered, framing her face from one corner of her lips to the other. Something about her features looked familiar—the shape of her green eyes. The man looked a bit older, with straight, graying brown hair combed over a bald spot. Again, something about his face seemed so recognizable. The suit he wore was expensively cut.

"Can I help you?" Anita asked politely, wondering what they were doing in this neighborhood.

The man spoke for them both. "We're Ruth and Warren Sutton, Larry Sutton's parents."

At the mention of Larry, Ruth's eyes glistened with tears.

Anita's heart skipped a few beats. "His parents? Larry told me his parents were dead!"

She was in absolute shock. Not only had Larry deceived her about affairs with other women but also he'd lied about something as basic as his parents. Why?

"Dead? No, we're very much alive," Warren Sutton said. "Here." He pulled out his wallet and showed Anita his driver's license. "May we come in?" he asked.

Flustered because she'd forgotten her manners, Anita's cheeks grew hot. "I'm so sorry. Please, do come in. The place is a mess, though. I'm moving tomorrow."

The Suttons exchanged a look, then stepped inside.

Marie was still playing with her activity box, chortling in glee when a new face popped up as she pressed a button or pulled a lever.

"Oh, how adorable!" Ruth exclaimed, going straight to the baby.

Protectively, Anita followed her.

"Hi there, honey," the woman said to the little girl. "Can I hold you? I'm your grandma."

When Ruth reached out to Marie, the little girl started to cry.

"She's shy around strangers," Anita said, picking up her daughter and holding her close. Motioning to the sofa, she suggested, "Please, have a seat. Can I get you something to drink?"

The Suttons were looking around with interest. "A glass of soda would be fine," Ruth said.

"Oh, I'm sorry. Since we're moving tomorrow, I haven't gone for groceries. I don't have soda. How about a glass of milk or orange juice?"

Again, the Suttons exchanged a look. "Orange juice will be fine."

For some reason, Anita got a chill when she thought about leaving them alone in her living room. She wasn't afraid they'd steal something, but...they made her decidedly uneasy.

Returning with the juice, Marie crawling after her, she sat in the armchair, her daughter on her lap. "You know that Larry's...gone?" Anita asked.

"We found out about a week ago," Warren told her. "Let me explain why you apparently didn't know about us." He rubbed his hands on his thighs and frowned, as if he didn't like the telling of the story. "Unfortunately, our son was in trouble a lot in high school. He ran off several times, not returning for weeks. He cut school whenever he wanted to and hung out with a bad crowd. Six and a half years ago, he didn't have a job or any prospects in sight. I wanted to kick him out of the house and show him some tough love, but my wife couldn't bear to do that. One night, drunk, he was in an accident that caused permanent injury to the other driver. We paid a settlement and ordered Larry to leave and not return until he could prove that he could be responsible."

A tear ran down Ruth's cheek and Anita felt so sorry for her.

"Surely he contacted you after he left?" Anita commented.

"No, he didn't," Ruth broke in. "That's what was so terrible. All these years, we waited for him to call us with an address where he could be reached. He never did. Then, about a month ago, something terrible happened. Some dear friends of ours had a daughter who was Larry's age. They'd gone to school together.

Paige got meningitis and died. Just like that! In two days, she was gone. Her parents were so devastated, and we were, too. It got us thinking. We wanted Larry to be a man. We wanted him to stand on his own two feet. But we never intended not to see him again. We never guessed he wouldn't come home."

"I had been stonewalling the idea of finding him," Warren admitted. "I didn't want more heartache for Ruth if he came back and hadn't changed. My pride got in the way of my role as a father. But then Ruth convinced me that finding our son was more important than my pride and we hired a private investigator. That's when we learned he'd been killed and that he had children—our grandchildren."

After Larry's death, after Anita had faced his infidelity, she'd tried to bury the betrayal. She'd tried to start over, determined to never put her future in a man's hands again. Now the past had been resurrected and the betrayal had resurfaced, making her ache at the thought of her own stupidity and Larry's lack of integrity.

"I'm so sorry you had to learn this way," she murmured.

"Do *you* have family, dear?" Ruth asked.

"No, I don't."

After a glance at her husband, Ruth gave Anita an ingratiating smile. "Why don't you tell us where you're moving to?"

"I'm taking a position as a housekeeper. Room and board is included for me and the children." She didn't like giving them too much personal information, but she also didn't want to be rude. After all, they did have ties to her children.

Just then, Anita heard the school bus rumbling down the street. Standing, she exclaimed, "I have to meet the boys outside. Today was their first whole day of school."

"Corey and Jared?" Warren asked.

At her look of surprise, he explained, "Their names were in our private investigator's report. Ruth thinks they are wonderful names. And we are very much looking forward to spending time with our grandsons."

As Anita picked up Marie and went outside to greet her twins, something in Warren Sutton's possessive tone sent another chill down her spine.

Chapter Three

An hour later, Corey and Jared were pushing trucks around the living room, bumping into boxes, as well as their sister, and making her squeal. The Suttons listened to the boys talk about their first day at school and their teacher and made small talk with Anita. Between comments on the kids, anecdotes about Larry and repeating the guilt they felt over losing him, they interspersed personal questions for Anita.

Ruth asked, "So is this Tate Pardell single?"

"Yes, he is," Anita admitted.

Ruth's lips pursed. "I see."

After Warren finished the remainder of his orange juice, he asked, "And you say you'll be moving tomorrow?"

"I sure will."

Taking a card from his inside jacket pocket, he handed it to her. "Would you mind contacting us and letting us know your phone number? We want to stay in touch."

Of course she wanted the kids to stay in touch with their grandparents. But something about the Suttons was making her uncomfortable. It was the way they looked at her, the narrowing of their eyes and the probing questions. "Sure, I'll let you know. Will you still be in town tomorrow?"

"No. We have to get back to Houston. I have a board meeting tomorrow. We're staying with friends in Tyler tonight, then leaving early in the morning." He rose to his feet and said to his wife, "We should be going."

Ruth went over to Marie and attempted to pick her up, but Marie backed away and crawled quickly to her mother. After a frown, Ruth crossed over to the twins. Although Anita had explained to the boys that the Suttons were their dad's parents, Corey and Jared had dismissed them unless they had been spoken to by one of them.

Warren tried to hunker down next to Corey, but his big stomach made it an effort. "I guess you boys will have to pack up your toys."

"Mom says that won't take long," Corey told him.

"You don't have room here for lots of toys, but I suppose you might where you're going."

Corey shrugged and Anita didn't add any information.

"I suppose you're still sad about losing your dad," Warren prompted.

Corey's eyes met Warren's then. "I wish I had a dad. But my dad never played baseball with us…like Mr. Pardell did."

Anxiety twisted Anita's stomach as Warren looked to her for an explanation.

"When Mr. Pardell stopped by to offer me the job, he played baseball with the boys for a bit."

"I see," Warren said again, and Anita didn't like the sound of his voice.

"Our son was good to you?" he asked Anita.

Anita was an honest person, and she wanted to tell the Suttons the truth. On the other hand, she didn't want to hurt them so she trod down the middle. "Larry wasn't here much. He often got home late or spent time with friends in the evenings."

"He didn't mistreat you, did he?" Warren asked gruffly.

After a slight hesitation, she answered, "No." How did you tell in-laws that their son had been deceptive and irresponsible and cared little about his family?

Five minutes later, the Suttons had left and Anita felt shaken. They'd assured her again that they wanted to spend time with their grandchildren, and Anita didn't know how that was going to come about. Houston was at least a five-hour drive from Clear Springs.

Marie pulled herself up onto Anita's leg and held her little hands up for her mom to pick her up. Lifting her, Anita held her close, anxious and worried without knowing exactly why.

When Tate called Anita around 7:30 p.m., he couldn't believe he was looking forward to the sound of her voice. He didn't react this way to women, especially not since Donna. He let the past rise up now to remind him not to be foolish or think a woman could be trusted.

Three days before they were supposed to be married, Donna had gone on an Internet spending spree to rival all others. Using Tate's credit card number, she'd ordered jewelry, purchased a new wardrobe and booked a holiday trip for them to Tahiti for a month after their honeymoon. He'd planned their honeymoon for a secluded resort on the Texas Gulf Coast, but she hadn't seemed excited about it.

The credit card company had called him because the purchases weren't in line with his usual pattern, and the creditor had suspected fraud. When he'd confronted Donna about it, she played sex kitten and purred that she thought he'd consider everything she ordered a wedding present.

Tate made enough money for a secure financial future, *if* he didn't blow it all. At the rate Donna expected to spend his money, he could never even think about retirement, let alone security. When he'd told her she'd have to send at least half of everything back—just to see what would happen—she'd thrown a fit. She'd tried crying first. That hadn't worked, so she'd gotten angry. She'd let it slip that she had a friend who worked at the bank and he'd told her what Tate was worth. If her husband-to-be couldn't see fit to spend his money on her, then she didn't see any point in getting married.

Tate supposed he'd been a lucky man. If Donna had waited until after they were married to start her spending spree, it would have been harder to extricate himself from their relationship.

Stuffing his hand into his pocket, he fingered the money clip Donna had given him for his birthday while they were dating. He should have seen the signs. He should have realized that money clip was a symbol of what she'd wanted from him. He'd handed over his heart, but what she'd wanted instead was his checkbook.

With his memories firmly in sight, he dialed Anita's number. She was going to become his housekeeper. Period.

But when she answered the phone, his pulse raced a little faster. "Anita, it's Tate. How does one o'clock tomorrow afternoon sound?"

There was silence until she asked him, "Are you worried about how this is going to look?"

"How what's going to look?" he asked, baffled.

"You being a single man. Me living there with you."

"We're not going to be living together, Anita. You're going to be working for me. It's not anybody's business." She'd been so gung ho about this job. What had changed her mind? "Are you having second thoughts?"

"I—" She paused. "I just never thought about how others might see it."

"Do you care?"

There was a new certainty in her tone when she answered, "No, I don't. I need this job. I'm not meeting expenses, and I don't intend to mount up more credit card debt. That's no future for my kids. One o'clock tomorrow will be fine."

Now she sounded like the Anita Sutton who had come into his office for an interview, determined to win the position. Yet something must have happened to make her think twice about the move.

"What happened today?" he asked her.

"Nothing. Nothing important."

The first part of her answer was a lie. The second part, probably a half truth. If Anita Sutton wasn't straight with him, she wouldn't be his housekeeper for long. Kids or no kids, pretty green eyes or no pretty green eyes, he'd been blind once, and he wouldn't be blind again.

He could hear her twins laughing in the background and realized how much he wanted that laughter in his house.

"Thanks for calling, Tate. I'll be packed up and ready to go at one tomorrow."

After Tate said goodbye and hung up the phone, he fingered the money clip in his pocket again, reminding himself to keep his eyes wide open.

When Tate came into his house from the corral, dusting his hands on his jeans, he felt something different in the air. His house was occupied by more than just him now. To his surprise, he'd found himself driving a truck to Anita's and helping two of his crew members pack her furniture into it. He'd also found himself helping to unload.

Afterward, she'd told him she would pick up her boys in about an hour, and that he should just go on with his day. She'd be fine.

Now, as he rounded the corner to her suite of rooms, he realized she'd done wonders in a short amount of time. There were no curtains yet around her sitting room windows, but throw pillows were positioned on the couch, the toy box had found its place in a corner and colorful rag rugs spotted the hardwood floors. Going to the first bedroom, he peered inside. Marie was sitting in the middle of the bed, holding a small pink blanket, sucking her thumb.

Beside the bed, Anita was struggling to lift a mattress into the crib.

"Here, let me get that." He was inside her bedroom before he thought better of it. Crossing to the far end of the crib, he helped her lower the mattress into it.

"Thanks," she said with a small smile. "Now all I have to do is find the sheets."

He glanced at the boxes against the wall, labeled in black marker. "You're an organized mover. I don't think that will be too much of a problem."

"When I was a kid, my mom and I moved around a lot. Not that we had that much, but I learned that if I didn't want things to get lost, I'd better know what I'd put in each packed box."

Crouching by the cartons, she studied her labeling, then undid the flaps on one of them.

"Why did you move around so much?"

She pulled out a sheet for the mattress in the crib. Tiny ducks danced all over the green cotton. "I wasn't sure why we moved until I grew older. Then I realized when Momma couldn't make the rent, we moved on."

"Is that why you want to pay your own debts? Your mother didn't pay hers?"

"Something like that," she replied offhandedly as she unfolded the sheet and flapped it over the mattress.

Catching the other end, Tate helped slip the elastic down over the corners. He knew he was prying, but he wanted to know more about her. "Where was your dad?"

Avoiding his eyes, she straightened wrinkles in the sheet. "I didn't have a dad. He left before I was born. My mother blamed him for everything that was wrong with her life."

"How did *you* feel about him?"

"He simply didn't exist for me. I was an accident— a one-night stand gone wrong."

"That's the way your mother made you feel?"

"Not intentionally. She loved me…in her way."

"How did she support you?"

Anita glanced over at Marie, who had laid her head down on the mattress, her blanket tucked under her cheek. Then her gaze met his. "Why do you want to know?"

On the same side of the crib now, they were only a couple feet apart. He could smell the wholesome scent that always seemed to surround Anita: vanilla. Was it a lotion or a perfume?

"I just wondered, that's all. Where we come from makes us who we are."

"I suppose that's true. You can either give in to it or rise above it. My mother was a maid in a motel."

"You were embarrassed by that?"

"No, but I always wondered why she didn't want more…why she didn't *strive* for more."

He took a step closer to her, and those couple of feet disappeared. "*You're* striving."

"I hope so," she breathed fervently.

As he gazed down at her, everything inside of Tate seemed to vibrate. She was altogether feminine and oh-so-pretty. He hadn't been with a woman for a long time. Donna had cured him of the impulse to jump into a relationship just to satisfy a physical desire. But he was wary of the way Anita made him feel.

"Something's different about you today," he said roughly. "You're distracted. *Are* you having second thoughts about this job?" If she didn't tell him the truth, if she didn't tell him what was bothering her, he'd be even warier of her.

After a few moments of hesitation, she finally responded, "It's nothing to do with the job and it's nothing for you to worry about."

"But it's something for *you* to worry about?"

"Maybe not. My intuition's just working overtime."

Turning away from him, she was heading toward the boxes again when he caught her arm. She had him curious now, and he wondered if that was her intent. "Tell me, Anita."

He saw the concerned look in her eyes and knew something was deeply troubling her. "I had visitors yesterday, visitors I never would have expected. Larry, my husband, told me his parents were dead. It turns out, they're not."

She still seemed stunned by it and Tate urged, "Go on."

"Larry lied to me during our marriage, so I shouldn't be surprised that there were more lies I didn't know about. But this—"

She sadly shook her head. "He'd apparently been in trouble as a teenager and his parents couldn't straighten him out. He hurt someone in a drunk driving accident and they settled it for him. But they disowned him. They told him not to come back home until he'd turned into a responsible man."

Tate gave a low whistle. "Saying your parents are

dead when they're not is one big, *fat* lie. How did his parents find you now?"

"A private investigator. And it troubles me that this man they hired seems to know a lot about me."

"If he was thorough, he could find out almost anything, especially on the Internet. What were these people like?"

"I'm not really sure. I became defensive when they started asking personal questions."

"For instance?"

"They could see I was moving. They knew I'd been a waitress. I told them I was taking a housekeeping position here. Then they asked if you had a family and if you were married."

"They had no right to grill you."

"Maybe not. But they seem to really care about their grandchildren."

"Where are they from?"

"Houston. They were staying in Tyler for the night and then going home today. They said they want to visit the kids, but I think it's more than that."

"How do you mean?"

"I think they feel guilty about Larry. I think they want to get *real* close to the kids. But I don't know how they're going to do that with them in Houston and me here. It was their glances at each other, the questions, the disapproval that was underlying it all that bothered me. I don't know. It's hard to explain. It just gave me chills."

"If they're in Houston and you're here, they can't interfere that much."

"I suppose not." She took a deep breath. "I have to go pick up the boys."

"Living out here, are you going to have to take them to school and bring them home every day?"

"No. I'll just take them down to the end of the lane. I already called the school and talked to them. The bus will be here tomorrow morning around seven-thirty."

Their gazes seemed to lock for a few seconds, awareness pulsing between them. Then she broke eye contact and crossed over to the bed. "Okay, baby. Let's change your diaper before we motor."

Changing diapers was totally out of Tate's realm of experience.

"Do you want an early supper tonight since you're home?" Anita asked him.

"Why don't we just order pizza? You don't officially start until tomorrow. That way, if you want to finish unpacking, you can."

"You're sure you don't mind?"

"I don't mind." He was beginning to realize that was the whole problem. He could picture them sitting around the table, sharing wedges of pizza much too easily.

"I'll be in the barn," he told her, going to the door. "Don't feel you need to tell me when you're coming and going. After all, we'll be living separate lives."

When she nodded, as if that was understood, he suddenly wondered how that could be true with them under the same roof.

They were soon going to find out.

Grateful for Tate's suggestion to order pizza for supper, Anita thought he might join them. Instead, he slipped two slices onto a plate and told her he'd take them to the barn. He had work to do there.

On his way out the back door, she asked, "Are you sure you don't want something to go with them?"

He simply called back, "I'll grab something else later." And that was that. Somehow, they had to figure out how to coexist while sharing the same house. With the sparks she felt whenever she was within two feet of Tate, avoidance was probably the best policy. However, in the past, avoidance had brought her nothing but a mess of trouble.

She considered that as she played a board game with the boys for a bit, and then got Marie and the twins ready for bed.

After she read them a good-night story, Corey asked, "Do you think Mr. Pardell would let us watch that big-screen TV sometime?"

"I don't know. I guess you'll have to ask him. But I don't want you running in there and playing with the remote on your own. We live on *this* side of the house. What do you think of your room?"

Both boys looked around at their familiar red-and-blue bedspreads, the poster of Curt Schilling on the wall and their toys in a large, plastic wash basket.

"It's okay," Jared answered. "I like having horses in the backyard."

Smiling, Anita hugged and kissed her boys, left the night-light burning and went to her bedroom to check on Marie. The baby was sleeping soundly, as if she didn't notice the change in location at all. How adaptable kids were!

She remembered her promise to phone the Suttons with her new phone number. She'd do that in the morning.

Thinking about Larry's parents brought back the rock in her stomach. It also brought back memories of the lies Larry had told her over the years—little white ones she hadn't paid attention to...that she'd avoided.

When she'd unpacked earlier, she'd stuffed a shoe box full of old credit card bills onto the top shelf of her new closet. Now she pulled down the box, taking it to the sitting room so that she wouldn't wake Marie.

Once on the sofa, she set it on the coffee table and opened the lid. She wasn't as organized as she should be with bills, but after Larry died, she'd sorted them into years. She took them from the box and laid them on the coffee table, staring at them as if they might bite her. She knew that by making only the minimum payment on her credit card bills, she was still paying for things they'd bought early in their marriage. Larry had always spent money quicker than he could make it. And the boys seemed to need shoes and clothes every couple of months because they grew so fast. Even when Larry worked steadily, they'd never had much extra income.

After Larry's death, she'd found a pattern in the charges. When he'd gone on a spending spree there were new clothes and haircuts. Also listed on the credit card statements were specialty items like flowers, candy and jewelry. Engrossed in her own life, run ragged some days dealing with the boys, waitressing and a new pregnancy, she'd opened the bills, paid the minimum and hadn't looked at much else. Now she realized that if she had, she would have had to confront Larry. She would have had to admit he was having affairs. She would have had to admit she'd chosen the wrong husband.

Had he ever really loved her? Apparently, promises had meant nothing to him….

Tears welled up. She felt the sadness and disappointment she hadn't let herself feel when she was married to Larry. She'd been young. He'd been older. The same year she graduated from high school, she'd lost her mother. When Larry had come into the restaurant—with his green eyes telling her he was interested, a smile that could coax one from her and compliments she'd soaked in like parched earth needing rain—she'd fallen for him. But she could see now that he'd never really wanted the responsibility of a wife and family.

As she thought about broken dreams as well as promises, the tears came faster.

"Anita?"

She hadn't even heard Tate come in. Quickly, she wiped away her tears and blinked hard but couldn't seem to stop.

"I'm fine," she said in a shaky voice. "Just fine. There's nothing wrong."

"The hell there isn't," Tate muttered as he quickly strode across the room and sat on the sofa beside her. "What's going on?"

"Nothing. Really. I was just looking through old bills."

"Old bills make you cry? Because you owe so much money?"

She tried another swipe at her cheeks and was more successful. Pushing her hair behind her ears and taking a deep breath, she looked down at the box rather than at him. "I was just realizing how naive I was. How blind I'd been."

Tate tentatively touched her arm, as if he didn't know if he should. The feel of his fingers on her bare skin sent an elemental jolt through her. Her eyes lifted to his and she saw that he didn't understand what she meant. "No, not because of money I owe. Because my marriage was a lie. I went into it for all the wrong reasons. And Larry…Larry went into it as if he were making a promise to change the oil in someone's car."

Understanding dawned in Tate's eyes. "I guess that means he was unfaithful."

"Yes, and I didn't want to see it. I ignored it. I turned away from red flags that should have blinded me."

"Fast courtship?" he asked.

She nodded.

"Got pregnant right away?"

She nodded again.

"How old were you when you got married?"

"I was nineteen. My mom died the year before and I was on my own, living in a room in a boarding house. When Larry came into my life, all the dreams I'd ever had suddenly seemed attainable. But I didn't really know him when I married him. Obviously, I didn't know him in our four years of marriage, either. I still can't wrap my mind around the fact that he told me his parents were dead and they aren't."

Picking up the credit card statement in her lap, Tate scanned the date on the top and his eyes ran over the charges. "You're still paying for gifts he bought another woman."

"At least there aren't any motel rooms on there," she said with a humorous laugh. "I guess he paid cash."

With a low oath, Tate put the credit card statement in the box, gathered up all the others lying on the coffee table, dumped them in, too, and then put the lid on. "You've got to forget about all this. It's not going to do you any good, wishing you had done something differently."

She knew he was right. "I wish I could forget about it, but I guess my pride still hurts. I guess I still wonder why I wasn't enough."

He moved closer to her. "Not enough? Enough of what? You're pretty and you're smart. You're a good mom, too. What more could a man want?"

That question hung precariously between them. Tate was looking at her as if he truly meant what he said. In jeans and a snap-button shirt, his beard shadow-dark, his blue eyes hot with a fiery spark that had pricked at them both since the moment they'd met, she couldn't turn away from him. When he reached out, took her chin in his palm and ran his thumb over her cheek, her heart skipped several beats. As his lips came closer to hers, she anticipated what was going to happen next. She realized she'd wanted it and longed for it ever since she'd met Tate.

When his mouth covered hers, nothing mattered but the sensation of it. Nothing mattered except breathing in his scent. Putting her hands on his broad shoulders and feeling the taut muscles there, the kiss turned wild immediately. Tate slid his tongue into her mouth and she held on tighter. The kiss was a roller-coaster ride, and she became breathless with the excitement of it, with the ascent of the passionate hill that promised satisfaction on the other side. The descent down that hill was tummy twirling as she kissed him back, feeling like a desirable woman again.

A desirable woman. Was that what this was all about?

The thought hit her hard, cutting through the passionate haze, striking her with the force of reality. When she pushed away from him, broke her lips from his, he looked a bit dazed, too.

"This is wrong. The last thing I need is another man," she murmured.

At her words, Tate's blue eyes became stone-hard, his expression tight with anger, frustration or something she couldn't even guess.

"That wasn't wrong, but it *was* a mistake." Standing, he announced, "It's probably better if I stay out of your rooms. I just came in to tell you I put the security system on for the night." He pulled a slip of paper from his jeans pocket. "There's the code. Memorize it if you can and tear this up. I'll show you what to do in the morning."

He didn't look back as he walked out of her sitting room and shut the door.

For a few moments, Anita couldn't help but stare at that closed door, feeling more lost now than she had earlier. Giving herself a mental shake, she knew she couldn't afford to feel lost. She had a life to build for her and her kids, and that was exactly what she was going to do.

Chapter Four

When Tate returned to his house from the barn Thursday morning, his kitchen was a foreign place. Marie sat in her high chair, banging on the tray while Jared and Corey chased each other around the table.

"Boys, sit down now," Anita called. "We have to hurry a little or you'll be late for your school bus."

Pushing and jabbing each other, the twins stopped their game and listened to their mother, noisily pulling out chairs and plunking down on them at the table, which was filled with good things to eat—scrambled eggs and bacon, toast, cereal and hash browns.

Anita glanced at Tate over her shoulder. "I was hoping you'd come in soon. I still have the coffeepot on. Did you have breakfast?"

"Just a glass of juice," he responded, almost feeling as if he'd landed in Oz.

"If you'd prefer peace and quiet this morning, I could serve your breakfast in the great room."

He'd always had peace and quiet. This ruckus first thing in the morning was a little jarring, yet when Jared grinned at him…

With fluid movements, Anita set a small dish with bits of scrambled egg on Marie's tray, next to a cup that was rounded at the bottom and tilted when the baby reached for it.

"The kitchen's fine," Tate answered. "No need to serve me somewhere else."

"What are you gonna do today?" Jared asked Tate.

Unused to conversation at breakfast, Tate pulled out a chair next to the boy and lowered himself into it. "I'll be working today."

"What kind of work?" Corey piped up.

"Well, for one thing, I'll be meeting with an architect who designs houses. He draws the pictures, and I make them happen."

"Wow! Neat!" Corey mumbled with a mouthful of eggs. "Do you drive a dump truck?"

Tate laughed. "No, one of my crew drives the dump truck. And a bulldozer. I used to, though."

Anita slipped into a seat across from him and encouraged her daughter to eat bites of egg, then met his gaze. The remembrance of their kiss was between them— pulsing and hot. The desire he thought he'd left in his dreams suddenly kicked him in the gut. When he'd seen Anita crying last night, he should have given her privacy and turned the other way.

Hopping up again, Anita reached for his plate.

"What are you doing?"

"I'm going to serve you breakfast."

Reaching out, he took the plate from her. "No, you're not. I serve myself." The idea of her serving him didn't feel right at all, even if she was his housekeeper.

"All right. But I think you'd better write up a list of the things I should and shouldn't do. Then we'll both be clear."

"It's not complicated. You cook and clean. That's it."

But one look into her eyes told him it *was* a lot more complicated than that, and she knew it, too.

Taking her seat again, she asked, "Do you want me to put some finishing touches on the house?"

"Like?"

"Curtains. Scatter rugs. Maybe a few pictures on the walls."

The condo he'd lived in before he'd moved here hadn't been very homey. It had a leather couch and a TV, and he'd spent more time at his office than there.

"Do you want to go to the furniture store and look around for what you need?" Maybe she just wanted to shop and spend his money.

"I don't think I'll find the things I'm looking for at a furniture store."

"So you'll need cash."

"I don't have to pick up everything at once. The process is what makes it fun. It'll give me something to do on my days off."

He needed to talk to her soon about planning the barbecue, but if he planned to have his employees over, he wanted the place to look decent. Pulling several hundred dollar bills from his money clip, he handed them to her. "If you want to get started, here you go. If you need me to open an account somewhere, just have the manager of the shop call me." He also pulled a business card from his wallet and handed it to her. "Those are my office and cell phone numbers. You can always reach me on my cell. Take the morning and find some things. Consider it part of your job."

"I was going to shop for groceries today. You have a good supply of meat in the freezer, but you need vegetables and I'd like to buy a few spices."

"You're the cook."

Although Anita's and Marie's plates were still half-full, Anita stood anyway. "Come on, boys. I've got to get you to that bus stop. It's such a pretty day out there. I'll put Marie in her stroller and we'll walk."

"You're not finished with breakfast yet," Tate said, although his was almost gone.

"The bus won't wait for me to eat breakfast," she joked.

"*I'm* leaving now. Why don't I just take the boys to the bus stop?"

"Are you sure you want to do that? You have to wait until it comes."

"Is it usually on time?"

She nodded. "It should be. They have a schedule to follow."

"No problem. I'm on my way out anyway. You and Marie finish your breakfast. I'll give you a call when the boys are safely on the bus."

Ten minutes later, as Tate sat with the boys in his SUV at the end of the lane, he turned sideways in his seat to peer back at them. "Do you think you boys are going to like it out here?" He'd had the backyard fenced in case he wanted to get a dog. Now he realized fencing would make the property safer for Anita's kids, too.

"We have more room to play," Jared said quickly.

"We can hit our baseball and not worry about breaking a window," Corey added.

Tate chuckled. "Yes, I guess you can."

"Can we watch your big-screen TV sometime?" Corey asked. "Mom said we had to ask you. We couldn't just turn it on."

From what he'd seen so far, Anita disciplined the boys well and taught them manners. "Sure, you can watch it sometimes. Just make sure your fingers aren't sticky when you use the remote," he warned with a grin.

"We never watched a big-screen TV before," Jared told him, adjusting his backpack. "Our daddy said he was going to buy one, but he never did."

It had been a year since their dad died, and with the boys only being five, Tate wondered how much they remembered of their father. "I'll bet you boys miss him a lot."

There was silence as they both seemed to think about it. "We didn't see him very much," Jared finally said.

"He worked a lot?"

The boys exchanged a look. "Mommy cried sometimes at night. When Daddy came home, he talked different."

"Talked different?"

"Yeah, slower. And he laughed a whole lot. But Mom didn't laugh with him."

It seemed kids picked up everything. Tate wondered

if the nights Larry Sutton had talked slower and laughed more, he'd been drinking.

They heard the grumble of an engine and the rumble of tires.

"Here it comes," Jared said, hefting his backpack onto his shoulders.

"Hold on a minute," Tate said. "I wouldn't want it to run you over." Out of the car in a flash, he opened the boys' door, watching over them as they went to stand by the mailbox.

When the bus door opened, they clambered on, but Jared turned and gave Tate a wave.

Tate found himself waving back. Then the bus was clattering down the road, leaving Tate with a funny feeling in his chest…a funny feeling he didn't want to examine.

After Anita put Marie in her playpen, where she'd be happy for a little while, she went outside and brought in all the packages. Then she stowed away the groceries and took everything else to the great room. This morning, Tate had surprised her by offering to take the boys to the bus stop. Whether he knew it or not, he'd be a great role model. Her twins needed one.

And what do you need? a small voice asked. *Another kiss?*

Tate's kiss last night had made her world spin. He was sexy and kind…

You don't know how kind he is, she told herself. *You really don't know that much about him.*

Would he ever lie, as her husband had?

Her gut told her no, but Larry's deceptions had

stabbed deep. She didn't know when—or if—she'd be able to trust another man.

Twenty minutes later, Anita handed Marie a bottle, sang her a lullaby and rocked her to sleep. After her daughter was settled in her crib, Anita found the sweeper in the closet by the utility room. She was going to clean Tate's great room, then show him the difference between a house and a home.

While Anita was running the sweeper, she decided to do the whole house. As she moved from room to room, she felt a little bit like Cinderella. She'd never been around such quality furnishings, such expensive carpeting, such a beautiful and spacious house. Sunlight poured in from the skylight in the hall, making shadowy places bright. When she came to the master suite, she didn't know whether to go in or not.

Convincing herself curiosity had *nothing* to do with her entrance, assuring herself that Tate had hired her to clean his entire house, she pushed open the door. The room was huge, with a king-size bed. The black iron headboard seemed to make it even more immense. The carpeting was sand-colored, and the comforter on the bed was shades of brown, rust and green. A heavy dark-oak dresser took up an entire wall, and the matching armoire rose practically to the ceiling. Jeans lay over a burgundy leather chair, while a book on bull riding sat on the hassock. There was a pair of fine, hand-tooled leather boots resting beside the armoire. Tate Pardell seemed to be a multidimensional man, but she warned herself not to be intrigued by him.

After vacuuming, she steam-ironed the curtains

she'd just purchased. Actually, they weren't curtains but rather scarf valances in a chocolate-brown faux-suede material. She'd bought rods and fixtures, too, as well as a small hammer. Now, using the kitchen step stool, she attached the hardware and began arranging the valances.

The window treatment set off the blue, tan and claret furniture in the great room perfectly, picking up the warm tones of the dark-oak cocktail table, end tables and entertainment center. The pièce de résistance, as far as she was concerned, was a leather rug she'd found at a flea market, along with two Southwest-patterned rugs she'd unearthed at a trading post, a few pieces of pottery and a bundle of dried flowers.

Spending a lot of time shoving the sofa and chairs this way and that, she finally came up with an arrangement she liked around the fireplace as well as the entertainment center. After hanging a grouping of cowboy-at-work prints, along with a copper-toned spirit horse, the room took on an entirely different character from before, and she liked the effect. She hoped Tate would, too. As a finishing touch she added three tan pillar candles to the mantel, along with a stone replica of a Zuni bear, which set off the Western flavor of the room.

Now all she had to do was wait for Tate's reaction.

Two hours later, when Tate parked in the garage and came into the kitchen from the hall that passed the utility room, Anita was cleaning up. When he hadn't returned home by six, she'd fixed him a plate and stowed it in the refrigerator.

"Hi," she said brightly. "Marie just fell asleep and the boys are putting on their pjs. Long day?"

It was almost eight o'clock and she wondered if he'd run into problems at work.

"Sometimes I get home later than this. I'm going to grab a shower. You don't have to hang around in here. I can warm up my own food."

She didn't know if he was just trying to be considerate, or if he didn't want to be around her. "I bought some things for the great room. Take a look on your way. Oh, and I swept the house. Including…" She paused.

"Including?"

"Including your bedroom. I assumed you'd want me to do that, too."

"Sure," he grumbled. "Of course you'd do that, too."

"If you don't want me in there—"

"It's not a problem, Anita."

But his attitude told her it might be.

While Tate showered, Anita read the twins a story and put them to bed. Afterward, she heard the beep of the microwave and couldn't help walking toward the kitchen. She wanted to know what he thought of her decorating touches.

"Dinner okay?" she asked.

He looked down at the roast beef, green beans and parsley potatoes. "It looks great."

"What did you think of the great room?"

"It looks…different."

"Different good or different bad? If you don't like it, I can figure out—"

"I like it fine."

His demeanor belied his words. "What's wrong, Tate? If you really did mind me going into your bedroom—"

"I don't mind," he said evenly.

Planting her hands on her hips, she asked, "Then what's wrong?"

With a sigh, he rubbed his hand down his face. "There were problems at work today. One of the crews put the wrong window in a house we're building. Another site is behind schedule. I had to put out fires all over the place and didn't get to some paperwork that needs to be done."

"And?" she asked perceptively.

For a moment she thought he wasn't going to answer her. Or he'd just wave off her poking. Then he admitted, "I'm having trouble getting used to our arrangement. I'm used to silence echoing off the walls."

"I think your bedroom or office would be pretty silent about now. I don't hear anything else going on."

After looking down at the plate of warm food in his hand, he set it on the table. "My last housekeeper wasn't a live-in. She cleaned but didn't care if my place was decorated or not. And her meals weren't as down-home good as yours."

"Don't the women you date cook for you?"

"Actually, no. I usually take them out."

"Oh."

Raking his hand through his hair, he added, "This just feels funny to me. It's almost like I have a family again. And I don't."

It was on the tip of her tongue to ask him if he *wanted* a family again. Instead, she asked, "How long has it been since you had a family?"

"I was twelve when my brother died. Everything went to hell in a handbasket after that."

Perfectly still, she was afraid he'd stop talking if she moved. "What happened?"

"It doesn't matter what happened," he responded with an edge to his tone, sitting down at the table and staring at the food.

She knew his history *did* matter. Something about it had hurt him, and hurt him deeply. But she couldn't pry it out of him, and she didn't want to. All the prying and listening in the world hadn't gotten Larry to open up to her. Maybe that was just the way men were. She hadn't had enough experience with them to know.

"I made vanilla pudding. It's in the refrigerator if you're interested." Turning away from him, she was heading back to her room when he asked, "Do you know how to make hors d'oeuvres?"

Facing him again, she admitted, "I don't have a lot of experience at it. We had a block meeting before Marie was born and I took along some tiny chicken quiches. Is that the kind of thing you mean?"

"I have no idea." Tate finally smiled at her. "It's like this. Every year I have a barbecue for my employees. In the past, Dorothy started out with hors d'oeuvres and then did something with ribs in the oven and then the slow cooker."

"She probably broiled them and then let the slow cooker glaze them."

He looked relieved that Anita knew what he was talking about. "She picked up salads at the deli, and we always bought sheet cakes at the bakery. I didn't expect her to make everything herself. The thing is, the date for the barbecue is coming up. It's usually the second weekend in September, which is about three weeks away. I was wondering if you thought you could handle it. If you can't, I'll have it catered."

"How many people?"

"About thirty to forty usually show up."

"I've never planned anything that big, but I'm willing to try. Three weeks is enough time to shop. I can make some of the hors d'oeuvres ahead of time and then just heat them up. If you want something other than the sheet cakes or dessert to go along with them, I could bake pies or batches of cookies."

"If you need to have Inez watch the kids, I'd be glad to pay her."

"Let me think about that."

"I'll give you a bonus, too, because it's going to be a lot of extra work."

If he was expecting her to argue with him, she wouldn't. She could use that bonus for Christmas presents for the kids. "We will have to discuss if you want the party inside or outside. You'll have to tell me exactly what you have in mind."

When Tate's gaze met hers, she saw what he wanted, what any man wanted—pleasure and satisfaction without a price tag. She'd be insane to get involved with him when he didn't even know if he liked having people around the house.

The current zipping between them was red-hot. Just as she was trying to decide how to make her getaway, Marie began to cry.

"Uh-oh," Tate said. "Does that mean trouble?"

Smiling, Anita shook her head. "She only drank about half her bottle before I put her to bed. Now she probably wants the other half."

On top of Marie's cries, they heard Corey call, too. "Mommy, Mommy, Jared says there's a monster in the closet. Come look."

"It never fails," she said with a shake of her head as she went to the refrigerator. "If it isn't one, it's three."

"If they're really afraid of a monster, I can check on that for them while you take care of Marie."

"Tate, the boys can wait—"

"I know they can. But this is a strange place for them. They're probably seeing shapes and shadows. I remember my imagination when I was a kid."

"All right. But don't let them talk you into reading another story, too. They can be conniving at times."

Chuckling, Tate said knowingly, "I already guessed that."

Tate wasn't sure why he'd offered to check the boys' room. The offer had been out of his mouth before he'd thought better of it. It wasn't as if he didn't have things to do. The horses had to be tended to yet. But just the thought of two little boys afraid of scary monsters created an urge inside him to reassure them...to make the world safe for them.

When he entered their room, he was struck again by how quickly Anita had tried to make it home. He also noticed she straightened up every night. He'd bet his best Stetson that she made the boys help.

As soon as Jared saw him, he said seriously, "There's a monster in the closet. I heard him."

Tate kept the smile from his lips. "Maybe something fell over in there. Or maybe the house creaked. It's new, you know. It might be settling into place."

"Houses do that?" Corey asked.

Tate shrugged. "Some houses do. Every house has its own particular noises." Switching on the light on the boys' dresser, he opened the closet door wide.

"Check in back of the clothes," Corey advised him.

Pushing back the twins' jeans and shirts, Tate ducked his head in, then ran his hand all over the back. "Nothing here, boys. Want to come see?"

"Mom says we shouldn't get out of bed once we're in it," Jared told him.

"Except to go to the bathroom," Corey added.

Tate couldn't help but laugh. "Well, I don't want you two to be sitting in your beds thinking I didn't check well enough. Come on, this will only take a minute. Duck inside here and see for yourselves."

After the boys scrambled out of their beds, they inspected the closet.

Satisfied, Corey asked Tate, "Can you look under the beds, too?"

"Come on. Let's do it together."

"But what if there's a monster there?" Jared asked.

"He'll see me and run the other way. I'm monsterproof."

The two boys looked up at him as if he were Superman. He couldn't believe the sense of satisfaction that gave him.

Five minutes later, the underside of the beds examined, the boys scurried back into their beds.

"How about a story?" Corey's eyes were as big and green as his mom's.

"Your mom warned me you might ask."

"We're not supposed to stall our bedtime," Jared told his brother self-righteously, and Tate was sure those were Anita's words.

"I'll tell you what. Instead of a story now, I'll read you one tomorrow night *before* you get ready for bed."

"Can we see the horses when you get home tomorrow night?"

"I don't know what time I'll be home. But if it's still light, I can give you a tour of the barn if you'd like."

The boys seemed happy with that, and Tate headed for the door. "See you in the morning, boys," he said with a tight feeling around his heart.

In part of his mind, he could envision roughhousing with them, teaching them to ride, hugging them after a long day. He didn't know what had gotten into him since he'd met Anita Sutton, but he wasn't sure he liked it.

While he'd been checking the closet for the boys, Marie had stopped crying. Going down the hall, he was just going to tell Anita that the twins were safely in bed once more when he stopped short in the doorway. A soft yellow light glowed from one side of the small dresser. Beside it, Anita sat in an old, caned rocking chair, holding Marie in her arms as she drank her bottle, humming as she slowly rocked back and forth.

The sight increased the tightness in Tate's chest and made it almost hard to breathe. Anita *was* a good mother—there was no doubt about that. She couldn't pretend her reactions to her kids or the way she handled them. They listened to her because she commanded their respect, not out of fear but out of love. They obeyed because they knew that she knew best. But what else did he know about her? Sure, she could cook and arrange a room so it felt like a home. That room had stopped him in his tracks this evening when he'd seen the changes she'd brought to it—the warm, colorful touches that had made such a difference, the effort she'd put into pleasing him. But he'd wondered what else she was going to change around here. He'd wondered if he wanted *any* of it to change.

She'd told him she wasn't in the market for another man, and that should be a relief. But she could have hidden motives. He didn't know yet what made her tick. He only knew the chemistry between them was troubling because he was finding it harder and harder to resist her.

Seeing her like this with her daughter—

"Tate, is everything okay?" She had stopped humming and was looking up at him now.

"Everything's fine. The monsters are driven out of the room."

When she smiled at him like that, he ached to do a lot more than kiss her, so what he was going to do was leave. "I have work to do in the barn. I just wanted to tell you it would be about an hour before I switch on the security system and turn in."

Marie was asleep in her mother's arms now. Setting the bottle on the floor, Anita lifted her precious bundle, carried her daughter to the crib and laid her in it.

He found he couldn't just walk away.

Anita tenderly brushed Marie's hair behind her ear, leaned in to give her a kiss on the cheek, then came to join him at the door. "Do you like what I did to the great room or would you rather I take everything back? I can, except for the leather rug."

After a slight hesitation, he admitted, "I like it all."

"I have all the receipts if you want to see them. They're on the kitchen counter. So is the change from the money you gave me. I didn't have a lot left."

"I can't believe it stretched as far as it did," he remarked.

"I know where to shop."

Most women did. Only it seemed Anita had looked for bargains, and he wondered if she'd done that to make a good impression or if it was just second nature to her.

The hallway light was on and its yellow beams played with the red strands in Anita's hair. The freckles on her nose begged to be kissed. Tate took a deep breath to remind himself to keep his guard up.

"Would you like hotcakes tomorrow morning for breakfast instead of eggs? Or both?"

Yeah, he'd like both. He'd like more than Anita's hotcakes and eggs. For that reason, he said, "I'll be skipping breakfast tomorrow. I have to be at a site early."

From her expression, he couldn't tell if she was disappointed or not. He couldn't tell if she cared or not.

She said softly, "I'll make hotcakes again this weekend. Then you won't miss out."

His refrigerator was stocked. His cupboards were full. Good smells lingered in the house, and he now had a great room he'd invite anyone into. So why was he feeling so unsettled? Why was he wishing Donna had never happened and he could look at Anita with unjaded eyes?

But he couldn't. The longer he stood here, the more he'd entertain thoughts and pictures that would haunt his dreams.

Moving out into the hall, away from her vanilla scent, green eyes and curvy figure, he called over his shoulder, "I'll see you sometime tomorrow."

"Tomorrow," he heard her repeat as he strode to the kitchen and then out the door.

Chapter Five

When Anita heard a horse trailer rumbling up Tate's long driveway, she scooped up Marie, who'd been crawling toward a stacking toy, and peered out the great room's large picture window. She'd been staying out of Tate's way, and he'd been staying out of hers. That had seemed the best thing to do during the past few days. He'd been away almost all day Saturday. She'd taken the kids shopping for shoes and school supplies on Sunday. And this morning he'd left before she'd gotten up.

There was definitely a buzz in the room whenever they were together.

Now, as she saw his SUV follow the horse trailer up to the garage and then around the back of the house, her pulse picked up its pace and she couldn't seem to slow it down.

Hormones, she told herself.

Loneliness, a voice whispered back.

Aloud she said to Marie, "I can't possibly be lonely with you three around."

But the truth was she'd been lonely since she was a kid. She'd always longed for a deep, soul-stirring connection to someone else and had never found it. But her knees going weak whenever Tate was in the same room had nothing to do with the soul.

Hurrying to the back door, she stepped outside into a beautiful day. It wouldn't be long before fall made its cooler appearance. The sky was robin's-egg blue, the clouds as puffy as marshmallows, the sun almost piercing in its intensity as it shone on Tate. His tan Stetson hid his face from her as he stood by the barn and spoke to a man briefly, then helped him unload two horses. They were gorgeous animals, gray with spots on their rump. Appaloosas, she guessed. She'd never been around horses, though a person couldn't live in Texas and not know *something* about them. Two of the animals ran in the corral, but now Tate and the other man led the two new ones into the barn.

On a whim, she started down the path through the fenced-in yard with Marie in her arms, murmuring to her little girl that they could both use some fresh air. As she approached the barn door, Tate stepped outside with the other man, who tipped his hat to Anita, then ambled toward the truck and trailer.

She watched as he climbed inside, expertly backed around, then left the property.

With his head cocked, Tate was looking at her quizzically. "Are you bored with housekeeping or just curious?"

There was a wariness to his tone she didn't quite understand. "Just curious. I have work to do on the computer, but Marie decided she doesn't want to take a nap today, so I've been chasing after her instead. I thought a walk outside might put her in a better mood for a snooze."

He motioned toward the barn. "Have you had a look around?"

What did he think she did? Went snooping when he wasn't home? "No, I haven't. Moving and getting in tune with my duties here has kept me busy. Besides, I have no business being in your barn when you're not here."

When he studied her, she didn't understand what he was looking for.

After a few moments, he gave a little nod and asked, "Would you like a tour now? I don't know if barn smells might help put Marie in a sleepy mood, but we can give it a try."

Marie cooed and babbled in her baby language, seeming to agree with the whole idea. They both laughed. Anita touched her head to her daughter's and kissed her forehead.

Tate frowned, then motioned her toward the wide-open door.

"It still smells new," she remarked as she stepped inside.

"Yep, and it's still clean, too. I figure about a month should take care of that."

The barn was immense. She could see it was divided into three sections with at least twelve stalls, an open area for storage and an enclosed room she supposed held the tack. The two new horses swished their tails and moved around, nibbling at feed in their trough now and then.

"They're gorgeous," she murmured, seeing them close-up. "Appaloosas?"

"Purebred mares. I'm hoping by this time next year, they'll have foals."

"Oh, the kids would love watching…" She stopped.

"What?" he asked, turning toward her.

"Nothing. It's just that we don't know what will happen a year from now. I learned a long time ago I could make plans, but when fate intervenes, the best strategizing doesn't mean a thing."

As they strolled down the walkway, Marie laid her head on her mom's shoulder and Anita's arm brushed Tate's. When it did, he glanced down at her. Their eyes caught and held and they stopped.

"About the barn, Anita."

"Yes?"

"I don't want the boys anywhere near it without me. Got it?"

There were shadows in Tate's eyes and she wondered what caused them. His mood seemed edgy today, and she thought it better not to ask. "They stick pretty close."

"Boys are boys," he mumbled.

Pushing her thumb into her mouth, Marie cuddled closer.

"She looks like she might be ready for that nap now," Tate said.

"I hope so. I have a client who wants Web site changes up tonight."

Tate tilted his head. "How many clients do you have?"

"Eleven. Possibly a few more. They've seen my work and e-mailed me about prices for getting their sites up and running."

"You want to turn into a computer techie?" he asked with a grin.

"No, I want to become a graphic artist. And I will *someday*."

Tate took a folded sheet of paper from his back pocket. He opened it and handed it to her. "Here's a guest list for the party. Do you think you could buy invitations and send them out in the next couple of days?"

"Sure, that's not a problem. I can make a run into town after Marie wakes up and put them in the mail tomorrow."

"I'd appreciate that, as this is short notice."

"I don't think anybody will mind. People usually like a good party."

"You're probably right about that."

"I made up two menus. Maybe later you can look them over and tell me which one you like. I'll have to start buying and preparing."

Leaning back against a stall, Tate crossed one booted foot over the other. "I'm going to hire someone to tend bar that day. I'll also put in for someone to help you serve. You can't be twenty places at once."

"You don't have to."

"I don't want to run you ragged."

Shifting Marie to her other arm, she brushed her daughter's wild curls behind her ear. "I'm used to waitressing an eight-hour shift. One party won't run me ragged. But having another pair of hands to help serve and keep plates refilled would be nice."

The barn was silent, except for the swish of a horse's tail. She grew warm as Tate's gaze drifted over her face and lingered on her lips. She still remembered his taste. She still remembered his strong arms around her all too vividly. In the stillness, she could almost hear the beating of their hearts.

Marie laid her little hand against Anita's face, then nestled her head once more on her shoulder.

"She is such a good baby." Tate's voice was husky as he looked down at the little girl, and Anita suddenly knew without a doubt, that he'd be a good dad. She'd seen him with her boys. Now the look in his eye said he'd cherish a daughter.

"I'd better take her back to the house while the mood is right." Turning away from Tate, Anita headed down the walkway, eager to put her daughter down for a nap, get to work and forget the tender look in Tate's eyes before she read more into it than was good for her.

Half an hour later, Anita sat at her computer, deciding on colors and fonts for her client's Web site. Her computer was by no means up-to-date. She'd bought it used for a song. When people got rid of their old machines, they didn't know what to do with them, and she'd put this one to good use. She was intently studying the screen when she heard Tate's footfalls and remembered what he'd said about entering her rooms.

She braced herself for the knock. When it came, she called, "Come in."

As Tate entered her sitting room, she could see he, too, was remembering what had happened there.

Gruffly, he said, "I thought I'd take a look at those menus. Or would you rather I do it later?"

"Now is fine. This is going well. I'll have it finished before Marie wakes up."

She'd pulled the papers from a folder and handed them to him when her phone rang.

"Go ahead and get it," he told her. "I'll study these."

As she watched Tate amble to her sofa, she couldn't help but admire his loose-gaited walk, his slim hips, his flat stomach. With a small sigh, knowing her thoughts would only lead her to trouble, she picked up the cordless phone and answered.

"It's me," Inez Jamison said.

"Hi, there. How are you?"

"I'm just fine. But what's going on with you?"

"Still settling in."

"No, I don't mean that. I mean what's going on in your life that there's a man snooping around your old apartment?"

"What man?"

"Don't know his name. I just know he was wandering around today, asking questions and talking to your neighbors."

"What kinds of questions?"

"Zoie Mitchell told me he wanted to know if you went out and left the kids here alone. She thought he might be from social services."

"Social services?"

"He didn't show any identification and I told her not to talk to him again. She's got some sense and won't. But not everybody's like Zoie. Old Mrs. Kellogg is a blabbermouth. Not that there's anything to blabber *about*, but you never know."

Anita didn't know what to do about a nebulous man who didn't even have a name or title. "The next time he comes around, if he does, call me. I'll drive in myself and find out what's going on."

"Are you sure you want to do that?"

"No. But I don't like someone asking questions about me."

"How's everything going otherwise?" Inez asked.

Glancing over at Tate, who was obviously listening to her conversation, Anita answered, "Just fine. I might need you to watch the kids the second weekend in September. Are you free?"

"There's nothing on my calendar. I miss you terribly, but I know you have to get on with your life."

"I'm not going to forget about you, Inez. We're going to be friends, no matter where I am."

"Sure, we will."

Anita could hear in the sound of Inez's voice that she didn't believe her.

Inez added, "Give Marie and the boys a hug. I'll call you if that guy comes around again."

A few moments later, Anita settled the phone in its cradle.

Tate stood and came toward her. "Someone's asking questions about you?"

"Yes. Apparently he's not giving his name or his reasons. I don't like it." Her voice trembled a bit.

Tate took another reassuring step closer. "What are you thinking?"

"I can't help but wonder if it has something to do with the Suttons. After all, they had hired a private investigator to find out what happened to Larry. Maybe now they're trying to find out more about me."

"Instead of talking to you themselves?"

"When I called them with the number here, Ruth said she'd be in touch soon. I thought she meant for a visit."

"Maybe she *did* mean for a visit. Maybe this man has nothing to do with them. He could be a salesman. Don't borrow trouble, Anita."

Looking into Tate's blue eyes, feeling her heart flutter, she wanted to forget about a strange man looking into her business. She might as well until she knew who he was and what he was doing. "You're right. If I keep worrying, my hair will turn gray."

Reaching out, Tate took a curl from along her cheek between his fingers. "Wouldn't want that to happen," he agreed, letting the curl float away.

Clearing his throat, he looked down at the menus in his hand. "I like the first one with the chicken wings and apple-raisin pie. But I'll leave it up to you."

In a swift move, he laid the pieces of paper on her keyboard and aimed for the door. "I'm headed back to the construction site. It'll be late when I get back."

"Your supper will be in the fridge," she said to his back.

With a backward kind of wave, he left her sitting room and closed the door.

Tate Pardell was a man of many facets and contradictions. But that didn't concern her.

Lowering herself into the chair at her computer, she went back to work, trying not to worry about things she couldn't control.

* * *

Over the past two weeks Anita had gotten used to being Tate's housekeeper. He'd worked late most nights and she'd concentrated on her kids, her duties and preparations for the barbecue. The day of the barbecue dawned bright and sunny. Tate came into the kitchen about fifteen minutes before the guests were supposed to arrive. "Those things you put on the tables look nice. I'm glad you suggested we set up tents and chairs out back."

"What did you do when you lived in a condo?"

"The complex had a community room and picnic area. I used them. But this is a lot more welcoming."

The smell of ribs and wings glazing in slow cookers and the scents of apple-raisin pie and oatmeal cookies rode on the air. Anita was glad Tate was pleased with her efforts. After all, she wanted to last in this job, didn't she? At least long enough to squirrel away some money.

"I'll set out hors d'oeuvres as soon as your guests start arriving. You'd better warn them that the chili dip is as hot as blazes or they'll get a surprise."

Tate laughed. "These folks are used to hot."

The message in Tate's blue eyes as he looked at her was hot. They'd been avoiding each other because they both knew that was best. Yet whenever they did come into contact, they couldn't deny the buzz between them. Today, Anita wore her best pair of black slacks and a white blouse. Tate seemed to be taking that in, along with everything else about her.

"What time are you going to pick up the kids tonight?" he asked.

"I told Inez the party would probably be over around nine o'clock. I don't want to bring them back here while you still have guests."

"I suppose that's best."

They still hadn't figured out a way to keep their lives completely separate, and she didn't know if they'd ever be able to. Nevertheless, she was trying.

The "Yellow Rose of Texas" began playing through the house and Tate said, "Here we go."

Ready to get the party started, Anita took the dips from the refrigerator, as well as the tray of vegetables. While she carried those out, Tate went to answer the front door.

Along with the bartender, Tate had hired a woman to help serve. In her late forties, Evelyn was pleasant and took Anita's directions easily. Some of Tate's guests brought their wives and others their girlfriends. For the most part, everyone seemed to have a good time, especially after Tate put on some music and couples danced on the patio.

As dusk fell, a few of the guests wandered inside and made themselves comfortable in the great room. Anita was about to take a tray of cookies in there when she heard one woman say to another, "The redhead is his housekeeper. But the way Tate Pardell looks at her, I'm wondering if she's not a lot more."

Anita stood in the hallway, her cheeks flushing, as she remembered Tate's kiss, as she thought about her own reaction to him. Even though he had kissed her—*once*—she *wasn't* more than a housekeeper, and she hated being the butt of conjecture. But whether guests were gossiping about her or not, she had a job to do here today. Squaring her shoulders, she carried the cookies into the great room with a plastic smile, offering them to Tate's guests. When the doorbell rang again, she was relieved. Setting the tray on a coffee table, she went to answer it.

When she pulled the door open, her stomach sank because she immediately recognized the man standing there—Kip Fargo.

"Well, hello there, Anita," the tall, blond worker drawled in his deep Texan accent. "Imagine seeing *you* here."

Before Larry was killed, Kip had been on the same crew as her husband. He'd come to the house to play poker several times. One of those times, he'd made a pass at her. She didn't much respect a man who would go after a married woman, and she'd told him so bluntly. Ever since then, his looks of disdain and anger got across the message that he didn't like his male ego being trod upon.

His gaze passed over her insolently as he asked, "How do you know Tate Pardell? Are you dating somebody on one of his crews?"

Kip wasn't the type of man she wanted to confide in, or even get tied up in a conversation with. "I'm working for Mr. Pardell. Won't you come in?" she asked politely. "Some of his guests are in the great room, others are out back. The food's out there, too."

"Sure, I'll come in. Can't wait to see this showplace. It makes you wonder what Tate Pardell did to deserve it, doesn't it?"

"I imagine he worked hard. Isn't that how everyone gets ahead?"

"By working hard?" Kip gave a humorless laugh. "Luck has a big part in it. I'll never get rich on what I make as a foreman for Pardell. I'm looking for something better."

Brushing past her, Kip stepped inside and began examining everything about the house. When he glanced into the great room, he gave a low whistle. "Everything must have cost a bundle." He glanced at Anita again. "Why don't you show me where the action is?"

If there was a double entendre intended, she wasn't going to acknowledge it. With her back stiff and her shoulders straight, she led Kip to the sliding glass doors in the dining room and opened them so he could join the other guests on the patio.

"Aren't you coming out?" he asked eagerly as the music and the guests' conversations swirled around them.

"No. I have work to do in the kitchen."

"You're a maid now?" he asked slyly.

"I'm Mr. Pardell's housekeeper." Turning away, she added, "Have a nice evening."

But Kip wasn't going to let her go that easily, and he grabbed her arm. "Now that Larry's gone, maybe you'll do the two-step with me."

Her stomach rolled at the thought of it. But she didn't want to antagonize this man who Larry had once told her could be a mean drunk. She didn't want to bring trouble into her life.

Before she could pull away, Tate seemed to appear out of nowhere, standing beside Kip. Both men were the same height, but there was no comparison. Tate had pride, confidence and integrity that Kip Fargo would never possess. That showed in the way he carried himself and how he handled others.

Now he looked down at Kip's hand on her arm. "Hi there, Kip," he said amiably. "Do you and Anita know each other?"

Pulling her arm from Kip's clasp, she suddenly felt self-conscious. But she didn't back away from the question. "Kip worked with my husband on a road crew."

"Sure did," Kip acknowledged with a smile. "Not only that, but Larry and I were poker buddies. Anita says she's your housekeeper now. If she's cookin' too, you're probably eating like a man should. Her corn fritters can make a fella's mouth water."

Kip always made Anita feel uncomfortable, and that was true a hundredfold now. She didn't want Tate to get the wrong impression. Didn't want him to think she'd flirted with the man.

After looking from one of them to the other, Tate motioned to the party outside. "Go ahead and enjoy yourself, Kip. There's plenty out there to eat."

"I'll make sure I have some fun," Kip assured Tate, as he tipped his Stetson to Anita and stepped out back.

Tate closed the sliding glass door behind him and stood alone in the empty dining room with Anita. "What was that all about?"

She peered through the glass door and saw that Kip was still watching them. Tate noticed it, too, and motioned her away from the doors.

"It was nothing," she responded, hoping to treat the whole incident diplomatically.

"You've got to stop telling me that, Anita, because I don't believe it. Were you and Kip Fargo lovers?" His voice held accusation and a roughness she had never heard there before.

"No! Absolutely not. I was a married woman. Kip doesn't respect any boundaries and he made a pass at me. I told him to jump in a lake and that was the end of it."

"Where did he make a pass at you?"

"Tate, this isn't any—"

"Yes, it *is* my business. He works for me. I don't like the man personally, but he supervises his men well and I don't have any complaints about his work. Still, if there's something I should know, I want to hear it."

"Kip made a pass at me one night when he was playing poker with Larry. He's the type of man who thinks all women should fall at his feet."

"And you didn't?"

"I *didn't*. I meant my vows to Larry. No matter what problems we had, I was committed to our marriage. If you can't understand that..." Her voice broke and she couldn't believe how much Tate's opinion meant to her.

Suddenly, his hand was clasping her shoulder. "I'm sorry. I didn't mean to push it."

She shook her head. "It's all right." Taking a deep breath, she moved away from his hold. "I'm going to start cleaning up."

"Did you get something to eat?" he asked kindly.

"No. I'll wait until I get the kids and bring them home."

"You can take time to eat now. You can even slow down and mingle a little."

"I don't think that's a good idea. That would be

confusing for your guests. I'm a housekeeper more than a hostess."

"Yes, but—"

The sliding glass doors opened and a woman stepped inside. She looked to be in her thirties, with long brown hair and a friendly smile.

"Hi, Sandy," Tate said. "Enjoying the party?"

"Garth is eating those ribs as if they're the last ones on earth." Her gaze fell on Anita. "Did you make them?"

"Yes, I did," Anita said softly.

Tate introduced the two women. "Sandy Finney, meet Anita Sutton. Sandy's husband, Garth, is a family doctor in town. He takes care of my crew when need be."

"We're both enjoying ourselves," Sandy assured him. "He can't stop raving about the food."

"That's thanks to Anita."

"Barbecue sauce out of a bottle?" Sandy asked.

"No, it's my own recipe. But if you'd like it, I'd be glad to copy it for you."

"That'd be great."

"You two have something in common," Tate said. "Sandy has twins, too. They're girls. Three years old, aren't they?"

"They sure are," Sandy said with a laugh. "Nobody ever told me there were terrible threes, just like there are terrible twos."

Smiling with sympathy, Anita offered, "When there are twins to get into everything, age three seems to last forever."

"You two will have to share war stories sometime. Anita has twin boys who are five," he explained.

"I can only dream of five," Sandy said with a sigh, and they all laughed.

Anita liked this woman. She liked her a lot. But even though Tate had suggested she mingle, she didn't feel comfortable doing it. "I'd better see to things in the kitchen. It was nice meeting you, Mrs. Finney."

"Call me Sandy."

"Sandy," Anita repeated. "If you need any refills out there, just send Evelyn in to let me know."

Tate's gaze was on her as she went to the kitchen.

You're his housekeeper, she told herself again. Even so, she couldn't forget being held in his arms.

Chapter Six

All evening, Tate watched Anita, trying not to but unable to stop himself. She seemed to be everywhere yet not anywhere. She had a knack for escaping notice as she filled serving dishes, made sure empty plates disappeared and generally kept things running smoothly.

He wasn't running smoothly. He'd stayed away from her over the past few weeks, avoiding her when he could. He'd kept their contact to a minimum because he knew what would happen if he didn't. Tonight, when he'd seen her with Kip Fargo…

Something inside him had detonated.

He didn't want her to be simply his employee. He wanted a hell of a lot more than that. But the situation was sticky. He didn't know if he trusted her—not completely, anyway, when it came to her ambition to get ahead. Yet he really cared about her kids, even the baby.

When the boys joined him in the barn, he felt as if he was doing something important, telling them about his days growing up on a cattle ranch, showing them pictures of the types of horses he intended to breed. Corey and Jared were curious and couldn't seem to get enough of everything—the stories, the attention, the rough-and-tumble play around the hay bales.

Whatever was happening to him, Tate knew it all had to do with Anita and her kids.

As he entered the kitchen, he could see the ceramic pot from the slow cooker soaking in soapsuds in the sink. Long serving trays—too big to fit in the dishwasher—lay lopsided on the drainer. Anita had the refrigerator door open and was shoving things this way and that.

When she heard him, she gave a large bowl one final poke, then firmly closed the door. "Not enough room," she said with a grin. "You have leftovers. I might not have to cook for a week."

"Everything was delicious. You know that, don't you? The guests raved about all of it."

"I'm glad."

Silence settled between them until she murmured, "I have to go pick up the kids."

Before she could elude him, he touched her shoulder. "Wait a minute."

When she faced him again, her pretty green eyes held questions.

"I want you to know that *I* know you've gone beyond the call of duty, fixing up the house and all. A couple of the wives asked if I'd had a decorator come in."

"What did you tell them?"

"I told them you did it. The truth is, until you moved in, this place was just a building with some furniture scattered about. Now it's a lot more."

"A few rugs and some color in the windows makes a difference."

"I'm not sure it has anything to do with the rugs and the curtains. It has to do with *you*."

He could tell his words surprised her.

"Thank you, Tate."

"I don't want thanks. I want—"

"What *do* you want?" she asked softly.

He had to ask her something one more time. "You and Kip Fargo. Nothing ever really went on between you two?"

Spots of color appeared on her cheeks. "I was a married woman, Tate." She looked angry that she had to explain again.

"Married women get sidetracked, especially if they're not happy with their marriage."

Turning away from him, she headed toward her rooms. "I think I've already told you too much about me."

This time, he wasn't going to let her get away. He wasn't going to let her keep denying the chemistry between them. Catching her hand, he tugged her around to face him. "I don't think you've told me nearly enough."

"If you don't believe me…"

Her eyes suddenly welled with tears and his chest tightened. Were they true tears? Why couldn't he forget Donna? Why couldn't he shake his doubts?

"I've learned women don't always tell the truth, just as you've learned men don't."

He could see her anger fade and her eyes soften.

All he wanted to do was make her forget about her betraying husband and Kip Fargo, who didn't understand the sanctity of marriage. He only knew one way to do that.

She was standing against the counter and he moved closer now, positioning a hand on either side of her. "Do you feel what I'm feeling?"

For a fleeting instant, he thought she was going to tell him no. He thought she was going to deny their attraction and lie to him. Then she simply nodded and murmured, "I don't think it's a good idea."

"You're thinking too much," he said huskily, moving closer still.

When Tate's lips touched Anita's, there was nothing else in the world that mattered except their kiss. Pressed together, her breasts pushing into his chest, their lower bodies intimately close, he didn't even think about waiting before he slid his tongue into her mouth. Instead of being surprised by all of it, she seemed to embrace it, just as she embraced him. Her arms reached around his neck and her fingers laced in his hair.

His groan was deep and primal and hungry. He didn't know what it was about Anita that encouraged him to dream dreams he'd thought had long since died. He didn't know what it was about her that urged him to hope again. He might have become more cynical over the years, but part of him still wanted a bond that would never be broken. His bond with his brother all those years ago had been a lifeline that made everything matter more. When that was severed, the light had gone out of his world. The day Anita had come into his office, sat down and told him she needed his job, a little of that light had returned. Anita and light and laughter just seemed to go together.

Or was he fooling himself all over again?

Shutting down the thoughts, he let physical need take over. As he explored Anita's mouth, his breathing became ragged and he was more turned on than he'd ever been in his life. Somehow, he felt as if Anita was the answer to a problem he'd never quite solved.

One minute, she was as involved as he was; the next, he felt everything shift. He felt her pull back. He felt her shut down, and he knew he had to back away.

Separating their bodies, he gave them both a couple of inches of breathing space. "What's the matter?"

"I have to go pick up my children. I have to think of them first, Tate. Always."

It was a warning of sorts. The heck of it was, he understood it. He didn't want their first time to be quick any more than she did. She meant more to him than a fast tumble, and he had to make her realize that. "I know your kids come first. They should."

When she studied him with an intensity he'd never felt from her before, he wondered how many doubts and how many memories of betrayal she was working through. They were a pair, they were.

"I'm not your type, Tate."

He almost smiled. "How do you know?"

Apparently, she couldn't find any humor in it. "I don't come from where you do."

"I don't think where we come from matters. It's where we are and where we're going that does."

"I work for you."

"I know, and that complicates everything. I guess I could fire you," he said teasingly.

"This job means more to me than…than an affair."

Searching her face, he could find no hint of ambiguity…no hint that she had an ulterior motive…no hint that she might be using the job to get to him.

"You're becoming indispensable," he conceded. "You don't have to worry about me firing you. And the rest… We'll figure it out. Why don't I come with you to pick up the kids? They might fall asleep on the way home and you'll have all three of them to handle."

"You don't have to…" she began.

"I want to."

For the first time since he'd known Anita, she looked scared. It was a fleeting emotion that was there in those big green eyes and then gone. What was she afraid of?

"We'll have to take my car. It has a car seat for Marie."

"Your car it is." If he drove it, he might be able to tell what was wrong with it. He'd heard it grumbling the other day, coughing and chugging sometimes. He didn't want it breaking down while she was out somewhere with the kids. He knew something about cars, and keeping Anita safe while she was in hers would be next on his list of things to do.

He couldn't ever remember caring about a woman's safety before.

"Can you teach us how to ride?" Corey looked up at Tate with big beseeching eyes a few days later.

"You're awful young," Tate answered, not wanting to deal with this request yet. Up until now, the boys had followed him around the barn, hadn't gone too close to the horses' stalls and had shown a healthy fear of the animals. That's what Tate had wanted. Every time he thought about the twins and horses in the same breath, he remembered his brother, Jeremy, and what had happened to him.

"I'm sorry, boys. I think you're too small to get on a horse just yet. When you're older, we'll see what we can do."

"How old?" Jared asked.

"I'm not sure."

The boys' smiles had turned to frowns. When Tate heard a shuffle on the walkway, he looked up to see Anita. She'd probably heard the whole thing.

Marie was holding on to her mom, looking all around. "What's going on?" Anita asked.

"Not much. The boys wanted to ride and I don't think they're ready yet."

Seeing the disappointed look on her boys' faces, Anita went over to them. "Mr. Pardell is a busy man. It takes a lot of time to saddle a horse, and afterward, the horse has to be groomed, too."

"But we could help," Corey told her.

"It's not the time," Tate said with a shake of his head. "They're just too young. They have no business being on a horse until they know exactly what they need to do."

His voice sounded harsh, and he realized all his feelings for Jeremy were still there. Setting his Stetson back on his head, he took a deep breath. "I'll tell you what, though. I have a few apples over here. We could feed them to the horses and you can get to know them a little bit better. How would that be?"

The twins were all smiles again and Jared even jumped up and down. "Let's feed the horses. Let's feed them."

"All that energy in such a little bundle," Tate mumbled.

Anita laughed. "Times two."

Apples lay stacked in a bin near the tack room. Tate sent Corey to fetch one, then taking out his pocket knife, he sliced it into four sections, giving each boy two of them. "Next time you come down to the barn when I'm here, if you remember to bring carrots, we can feed them to the horses, too."

Tate never took his eyes off the boys as he let Corey go first and feed Pewter Lady. He made sure the boy was careful. "No quick movements now. You'll scare her."

"She's so big," Corey exclaimed. "She's got big teeth," he remarked with glee as the horse licked the slice from his palm and then chomped on it. "That tickles," he said with a little wiggle.

Seconds later, Jared marched right up beside Corey to take his turn, only he fed the bay. Tate brushed his hand through the horse's mane as the mare gobbled up the apple from Jared's flat palm.

"That's their snack for the day." Tate was glad the boys had listened so carefully and followed his instructions.

With the allure of the horses over now, Jared asked his mom, "Can *we* have a snack?"

She laughed. "I think your appetites are as big as those horses'. Go on up to the house and wash your hands. With soap," she added. "I made peanut butter cookies this morning. They're in the cookie jar. Two each. I'll pour the milk when I get there."

After they rushed through the barn door, she turned to look at Tate.

"Mama, Mama, Mama," Marie babbled.

Anita lifted the baby high in the air, wiggled her a little bit to make her giggle, then settled her in the crook of her arm again.

"You really think the boys are too young to ride?" Anita asked.

"They're way too young," Tate said firmly.

"When do you think is an appropriate age to start?"

"I don't know. Maybe when they're teenagers."

She cut him a surprised look. "When did *you* learn to ride?"

With some chagrin, he admitted, "When I was about four. But it was way too soon. And kids should never be allowed to take horses out alone. Not *ever*." The vehemence in his tone gave too much away.

"Are you so set against it because you got hurt?"

"No, I didn't get hurt." He wished he had. He wished it had been him the horse had thrown, not Jeremy. Then he wouldn't carry the guilt he did. *He'd* been the older brother. He should have known better than to let Jeremy gallop across that field as fast as the wind. If only something hadn't startled his horse…

Tate had lived with "if only" far too much of his life.

With Anita looking at him curiously and Marie staring up at him with the same green eyes as her mom, he suddenly felt claustrophobic in the huge barn. "I've got work to do," he grumbled.

"All right. I have boys to feed."

As she turned to go, he called after her. "Anita."

She stopped.

"I meant it when I told you I don't ever want those boys down here without me. Do you understand?"

"Sure, Tate. I understand."

But he could see she didn't. Not exactly. That didn't matter. She was a good mom, and the twins listened. They'd be safe as long as they followed his instructions.

When Anita left the barn, he breathed a sigh of relief. Thank God she had kids. They were good buffers—and great chaperones. If they hadn't been around, he'd have kissed her again, maybe pulled her into one of the stalls and made some of his fantasies come true.

And he was pretty sure that making his fantasies come true would land him in a peck of trouble.

That evening, after Anita put the baby and the boys to bed, she went to the kitchen to remove meat from the freezer to thaw for the next day's meal. Tate had gone to get the mail after he'd come in from the barn. On the counter, she saw two envelopes addressed in her name.

The first was last month's electric bill, and she put that aside for the moment when she realized she'd never before seen the return address on the other envelope. It was from a lawyer's office in Houston.

Everything inside her froze.

At that moment, Tate came into the kitchen, freshly showered. His hair was damp, and his shirttails were still not tucked into his jeans as he went to the refrigerator for the carton of orange juice.

"Kids all asleep?" he asked, lifting it out.

"Yes." She knew her voice didn't sound natural. She was afraid to open the letter in her hand.

Turning from the refrigerator, setting the orange juice on the counter, he asked, "What's wrong?"

"I'm not sure anything is yet. But I got a letter from a lawyer in Houston."

He could see she hadn't opened it.

"It might just be some kind of advertisement."

"Wouldn't *that* be a coincidence," she murmured, then slid her finger under the flap and tore open the legal-size envelope.

As she read the words, a sinking sensation in her stomach made her nauseous and she felt as if the room were spinning.

"Hey, there." He took hold of her elbow. "You're awfully pale. What's wrong?"

"It's from…it's from the Suttons' lawyer. They intend to sue for custody of the twins and Marie. Apparently, from the P.I.'s report, this lawyer has made a case. They think I'm unfit. He lists 'previously living in a poor neighborhood with not many material possessions, a low income, no health insurance and—'"

"And?" Tate prompted.

"And my moral fiber is in question since I moved in with a man I'm not married to."

When she started to shake all over, Tate must have felt it, too. Guiding her to the table, he pulled out a chair for her.

Swearing a string of epithets he'd picked up in the rodeo chutes, he sat down at the table beside her and took her hand. "You've got to stay strong, Anita. You can fight this."

"So you think it's serious, too."

"I do. And I think you have to know what you're dealing with."

She shook her head as if to clear it. "I don't know what you mean."

"I mean that we need to do a little bit of investigating on our own. There's a P.I. in town. I built a house for him."

"I can't afford that, Tate."

"He might do this as a favor to me. I don't think it'll be too difficult to find out something about these people."

"Mr. Sutton said he's on some kind of board. They couldn't stay in town because he had to return to Houston for a board meeting."

"Okay. His name is probably listed somewhere in a directory. I'll go call the private investigator and we'll see what we can find out."

She could hardly absorb what Tate was saying. She still felt shaken, as if her world had come tumbling down around her. This time, she had no idea how to build it up again.

As Tate left her there at the table, she didn't move—she just stared at the letter.

A few minutes later he was back. She didn't even realize she was crying until Tate pulled her up out of her chair and put his arms around her. "It's going to be okay."

With her face against his shirt, she knew nothing might ever be okay again. "How long will it take for him to find out anything?"

"Vic says he'll know something by tomorrow morning. Like I said, with computers, it doesn't take long."

Tears continued to run down her cheeks. "Tate, what am I going to do?"

"You're going to stand up strong and tell these people you're those kids' mother. Nobody is taking them away from you."

His voice was filled with so much indignation and so much certainty that she looked up at him and finally found her composure. "Thanks for the vote of confidence."

"You're a good mother, Anita, and any judge would have to see that. Any judge who wouldn't doesn't belong on the bench."

"Apparently, the Suttons don't think I'm such a good mother."

"This has nothing to do with them thinking you're a good mother or not. They feel guilty as hell about their son and what happened to him—that they didn't look for him sooner, that they threw him out. They're trying to make up for all of that by taking his kids. If *I* can see that, any judge worth his salt will see it, too."

"You haven't even met the Suttons."

"No, but I know what guilt is. I know that they're feeling it."

Tate's comment caught Anita off guard. But in the situation she was in, she didn't feel she could probe for personal information.

"Are you sure your friend isn't going to charge you?"

"He's not a friend. He's a business acquaintance. In small towns, we help each other out. Just like you and Inez."

"I should have taken Inez's warning more seriously. The man who was asking questions around the neighborhood must have been the Suttons' private investigator. I should have seen this coming."

"I think you did, but the idea of it was so big, you just couldn't look at it."

"It's still too big to look at."

Hugging her close, he mumbled into her hair, "You have to be realistic, Anita. We have to get the facts so we know what we're facing."

He'd used the term *we* and it surprised her. She'd expected him not to want to get involved. After all, this wasn't his problem.

Staring up into his eyes, she saw that he was going to make it his problem. That was such a relief that she almost started crying again. Instead, she concentrated on the strong contours of his face, the masculine set of his jaw, the forelock of hair that always tumbled down his forehead. He was a virile, handsome man, and she was so susceptible to that light in his eyes…a light that told her he wanted her.

When his mouth came down on hers, she felt every sensation as an escape from her uncertainty. She was learning that Tate's kisses were never easy, were always demanding and created a response in her that was so strong she couldn't hold back if she wanted to. Even now. Especially now, when her world seemed topsy-turvy. Tate was a solid bulwark she could hold on to. When she wrapped her arms around his neck, he pressed in closer, plumbing deeper into her mouth, angling his body intimately against hers.

What would a night in his bed feel like? She could imagine sleeping in his arms all too well. She could imagine waking up with him and starting the day with him. She was falling in love with him!

That realization, on top of everything else, was almost her undoing. Sliding her arms from his neck, she pushed against his chest and broke the kiss.

She couldn't speak—just stared at him—letting the realization sink in.

A little wryly, he said, "I guess you forgot about the Suttons' lawyer for about two minutes."

Had he planned the kiss to distract her? Was she just a convenient experience? Or did he feel anything at all?

"I've got some thinking to do," she murmured, backing away.

"Just so long as it's thinking, not worrying. Worrying won't do you any good at all."

"You could shut off all of this so easily? You think I'm going to get any sleep tonight?"

"I don't know if I *could* shut it off. But I do know you need to get some sleep to face whatever's coming."

Whatever was coming, she couldn't let feelings for Tate muddle her life more than it already was. She couldn't let a man's desire delude her into thinking he had feelings for her. Her father's desertion and Larry's betrayals had taught her well. Don't trust a man farther than you can see him.

Crossing to the counter, she picked up both envelopes. "Will you call me tomorrow as soon as you know something?"

"I'll call you," he said somberly.

When she went to her living quarters, she was still trembling. She didn't know if it was a reaction to the letter or to her kiss with Tate.

Chapter Seven

It wasn't even 10 a.m. when Anita heard Tate's truck crunching on the stone driveway. He'd said he'd call her with his P.I.'s report, not give it to her in person. Now her nerves became even more jangled. Settling Marie in her playpen, she waited for him in her sitting room.

Two minutes later he was there, looking grim.

"What did you find out?" she asked, holding her breath.

The brim of his Stetson was low over his eyes and he had to get close before she could see them. "It's not good. Warren Sutton is a banker and has connections. Apparently, they're an influential family in Houston. It didn't take much digging to figure out that he usually gets what he wants. Your husband was never charged for that accident he had. The settling was done privately. Not just anyone can pull strings like that."

The pounding in her temples grew louder. "What are you telling me?"

"I'm telling you that the Suttons have the kind of influence that can sway a judge. Even with solid legal representation, it's going to be a dirty battle and I'm not sure you can win."

"I've *got* to win! I can't lose my children!" She knew her voice was near panic. She couldn't believe that her world and his confidence had shifted so drastically overnight.

"I'll leave before any of this starts," she decided, determined to keep her children no matter what. "We'll head to Alaska if we have to and the Suttons will never find us."

Suddenly, Tate was even closer, taking her by the elbows. "Be realistic, Anita. You can't go on the run with three kids. What kind of life would that be for you and for them? Eventually, something would surface. Even if you don't use credit cards, there'd be some kind of record of bills."

She could hardly get out the words. "What am I going to do?"

When he went very quiet, she saw something in his blue eyes.

"What? Do you have an idea?"

"Yes, I do. The way I see it, if your life was more stable, they wouldn't have any complaints against you. I have a feeling it might be your current living situation that they're going to question the most."

She blushed and said, "They have no right—"

He cut in quickly, as if he had to get a solution on the table. "They don't have a right, but that's what they'll do. Only one thing is going to fix all of this. If you marry me, that would wipe out their case entirely."

As she breathed in the scent of his aftershave—the scent of Tate—it took a few seconds for his words to sink in. When they did, she couldn't believe she'd heard them. "Marry you? You can't be serious!"

"I'm very serious."

She could see that he was. He hadn't said it in joking. As she thought about it and gazed into his blue eyes, she felt her insides starting to quiver. "Why would you even consider marrying me?"

"Let's face it, Anita. You and I have both been fighting this attraction between us. It would be a hell of a lot more fun to give into it."

"You want to marry me for the sex?" That seemed ludicrous to her since Tate Pardell could have any woman in Texas he wanted.

His complexion became a bit ruddier and he dropped his hands from her elbows. "No, not just the sex. I didn't mean that the way it sounded. Look, my family broke apart when I was a kid, and I haven't had one since. I didn't think I cared. I believed being alone wasn't so bad. But then I started spending time around you and your kids. And it made me realize what I've been missing. I think marrying you would be the right move for me. You'd get the security you need and I'd get a ready-made family. My lawyer would set up a prenuptial agreement—"

"A prenuptial agreement?"

"Yeah. A prenuptial agreement. He would set up the terms if we ever split."

She knew, of course, that Tate Pardell had money. She supposed it would be only fair that he'd want to protect it.

Yet asking her to sign a prenuptial agreement also meant he didn't trust her. She didn't care about his money. In fact, the only reason she'd consider marriage to him was her deepening feelings for him. She'd woken up this morning even more in love with him. But what would she be setting herself up for here? He would be the rescuer and protector but might never really love her....

Could she handle that?

Apparently seeing the doubt swirling inside of her, Tate said, "I know this is a lot to absorb. I, at least, had the drive over here to think about it. You think about it, too."

"Tate, I can't believe you'd really offer to do this. Are you sure you even want to consider it?"

After a few interminable moments, he answered, "It's not as if we're complete strangers, Anita. Nothing much would change from the way it is now. Except the nights. And if, after the danger's past, either of us wants out of this, we can get out. I'm a practical man, and this is a solution to your problem."

Checking his watch, he headed for the door. "I've got to get back to the job site."

Before he could leave, she stopped him. "Whether we decide to do this or not, I want to thank you for offering."

He seemed embarrassed by her gratitude. "No thanks necessary. When we're both ready, we'll talk about it some more."

After Tate left, she bundled Marie into her arms and kissed her sweet neck, kissed her little cheek. Anita had never been more scared than she was at that moment.

But the idea of marrying Tate almost made the fear go away.

* * *

As Tate made his way through the house the following evening, he thought about how a man's life could change in a few days. Last night, before turning in, he'd assured Anita again that he'd meant his proposal. But she hadn't grabbed at the opportunity to marry him. Her hesitancy led him to trust her a little more. At work today, he'd been convinced they should get hitched. He hadn't made the offer to marry Anita just out of a sense of nobility. Once he'd thought of it, it seemed like a great idea and now he intended to convince her that marriage was the best course.

When Tate walked into the laundry room and spotted Anita folding his underwear, he knew he'd asked her to marry him because he wanted her in his bed. But also, he'd asked her to marry him because he wanted to be a father to her kids. With Anita, he knew what he was getting, plain and simple. That beat having to fence and duck and maybe even sic a private eye on any woman he intended to have a serious involvement with.

He'd seen the look on Anita's face when he'd mentioned the prenuptial agreement. There was a decided lack of trust on both their parts. Maybe they could earn each other's trust slowly. He knew what fidelity was and didn't intend to step out on her as her husband had. Maybe in time she'd learn he kept vows he made.

When he glanced at the underwear and then at her, her cheeks reddened. Moving toward her, taking a T-shirt in his hands and folding it himself, he said, "Sorry I'm so late. It couldn't be helped. Problems seem to be a dime a dozen this year."

"You don't punch a time clock with me, Tate."

"No, I don't. Have you come to any conclusions about my proposal?"

Avoiding his gaze, she just kept folding. "I got another letter today. It came by overnight courier. A court date's been set."

Tate whistled low. "That was fast. Somebody's got clout."

She lifted worried eyes to his. "Yes, and we know who, don't we? Before that letter came, I was thinking I could take awhile to make a decision. But now, I don't see that I can."

"What have you decided?"

"If I marry you, I can keep my children. But I need to know something. What kind of marriage would you expect to have?"

"I already told you the nights would change. I'm not doing this out of the goodness of my heart, Anita. I want the real deal. I want all the advantages of marriage, which means having you in my bed every night. I also want a ready-made family. That's the point of this whole thing."

Stepping close to her, he took his underwear from her hand and laid it on the dryer. Then he enfolded her into his arms and brought her close—so close his breath met hers. "Don't *you* want a real marriage?"

"My experience with a real marriage wasn't the best," she admitted breathlessly.

"I know it wasn't. But we can be partners in this."

Gazing into his eyes, she said, "You don't trust me. That's why you want me to sign a prenuptial agreement."

He couldn't deny it. "A prenup will safeguard both of us. You'll know exactly what you'll get if we split up. And I promise you, if you're straight with me, I'll provide for your kids, no matter what."

As he raised the stakes, he realized why he had. Her answer meant more to him than he wanted to admit.

"You mean you'd help them through school?"

"That's exactly what I mean. If something happens and this doesn't work out, their education would be part of the settlement. What more could you ask for?"

There were shadows in Anita's eyes. Anxiety. Concern. He'd give half his bank account to know exactly what she was thinking right now.

"So this will be like…a business arrangement?"

"With lots of benefits," he added slyly.

One more thing would push her over the edge and convince her. Bending his head, he gently set his lips on hers.

After a bit of pressure and settling in, he pulled her closer, slid his hand down her back, then breached her lips. With a soft sigh, she gave into the kiss and surrendered to him. He wanted her to not only need this marriage but also to *want* this marriage. Letting the passion grow, he stoked the flames until he was ready to strip off both their clothes. But then he stopped. If he pushed too hard, if he went too far, a woman like Anita might back away. Although his body was screaming for satisfaction, he knew courting was part of this whole process. Theirs had to be rushed, but it could still be done. By the time she slept with him, she'd want sex as much as he did.

When he broke the kiss and pulled away, she looked surprised. "I won't rush you into anything you're not ready for. I can promise you that. I'm a patient man when I want to be. But we'll get married as soon as we can so we can get that court date canceled."

"How are we going to do that?"

"By retaining a lawyer and notifying the Suttons that we're man and wife. Once they know that, they'll back off because there won't be any basis for them to take over custody."

Her expression was clouded with worry. "I hope you're right."

"You still haven't officially given me your answer."

He could see she was torn, that this wasn't what she had planned at all. That gave him some hope. Maybe she'd never had ulterior motives.

Finally, she declared, "I'll marry you, Tate."

The knot of tension in his chest eased and he was filled with a jubilance he hadn't experienced in years. "Great! I'll call my lawyer and get the ball rolling. Maybe you can ask Inez to stand up for you."

"Maybe I can."

But Anita didn't look happy when she said it, and he wondered exactly what kind of marriage they *were* going to have.

Anita wore her one good dress to her wedding. It was an all-season dress in a pretty green with three-quarter sleeves and a sweetheart neckline. She'd had it for a few years. Tate was dressed in a Western-cut charcoal suit and wore a bolo tie, the slider in the shape of Texas. With an ash-gray Stetson, he was more handsome than any man she'd ever seen. Even so, as they stood before a justice of the peace—Inez to her right, holding Marie and the twins beside her, Tate's friend Garth, who Anita had met at the barbecue, beside him—she wondered if she was absolutely crazy. What did she really know about Tate Pardell?

A lot, she had to admit, and she was learning more every day…falling more in love with him every day. That was the main reason she was doubting this wedding. How would this marriage work with her loving him but him not loving her? When she thought about the prenuptial agreement, Tate's lack of trust saddened her.

Still, as she said her vows, she knew she was protecting her children and her right to be their mother. That was all that mattered right now.

Since Garth was a doctor with a busy family practice, they had decided to get married in the evening. As the justice of the peace declared, "I now pronounce you husband and wife," Tate took her in his arms to kiss her. The kiss was a solid, no-nonsense one, and when they broke apart, she realized everyone was staring at them.

"That's mushy," Corey mumbled.

"That's romantic," Inez debated him with a smile, jiggling Marie, who was becoming restless.

With a grin, Garth clapped Tate on the back. "Congratulations, buddy. I never thought it would happen."

A look passed between the two men that Anita didn't understand.

"Can we have wedding cake now?" Jared asked.

Anita had to smile. When Tate had picked up Inez, she'd been carrying a large cake holder.

"Are you all going to come over to the house and have some with us?" Tate asked.

"I think you should go home, put the kids to bed and have a private celebration," Garth suggested. "To add to that, I brought a bottle of champagne for you. I can take Inez home, if you'd like."

"There's no need," Anita said quickly, not knowing if she wanted to be alone with Tate just yet, not knowing what was going to happen after the children were in bed for the night.

"Sure, Garth, you can take me home," Inez agreed. She transferred little Marie to Anita's arms. "There's no use you two wasting one minute of your wedding night."

Anita felt decidedly embarrassed about the whole subject.

"Mom, your cheeks are gettin' bright red," Corey pointed out, to Anita's chagrin.

"Kids see everything," Tate murmured. "For that reason, we're going to have to do a good job with this marriage."

A good job, Anita thought sadly. That's the way Tate thought of it.

Half an hour later, back at Tate's house, the boys sensed something different in the air. While Anita got Marie ready for bed, Tate fed the boys slices of wedding cake. As she gave Marie a bottle and rocked her, she could hear Corey and Jared chattering with Tate in the kitchen and heard his deep voice answering them. He was so comfortable with them and talked to the twins as if they had some sense. Larry hadn't known how to relate to them and had been awkward, barking orders, expecting them to be seen and not heard. Tate seemed to understand that boys needed to be rowdy now and then.

After Anita kissed her daughter and settled her in the crib, she found the twins dressed in their pajamas, sitting on their beds. Tate had discarded his suit jacket and tie, and was sitting at the foot of Jared's bed, reading them a story.

Standing just inside the doorway, she waited until he finished.

Afterward, she crossed over to her sons, pulled up their covers and kissed each one on the forehead, aware all along that Tate's eyes were on her.

"Mr. Pardell says we can call him Tate now," Jared announced.

"He says your name's different than ours. Is that so?" Corey asked, looking confused.

"Yes, my name's going to be different now. I'm Anita Pardell."

"But we want the same name as yours," Jared complained.

"Oh, boys...."

"Maybe we can do something about that," Tate said, his eyes holding hers. "But it'll take a while."

"How long?" Corey asked.

"I'm not sure. I'll look into it. But it can be a year or so, I bet. The thing is, boys, if you get the same name as mine, that means I'm officially your dad. Is that what you guys want?"

Corey and Jared's silent consultation took a few moments, then both of them looked at him and nodded.

Tate cleared his throat. "Your mom and I will talk about it. For now, you get some shut-eye."

A few minutes later, Anita followed Tate down the hall and into the kitchen. "Tate, I never expected you to adopt them."

"Don't you want me to?" he asked.

"I hadn't really thought about it. All of this happened so fast. Maybe you should wait and make sure you *want* to be a father."

"Maybe what you're really saying is, you want me to wait so *you* have time to see if *you* want me to be their father."

"I guess we all need time to absorb this."

Instead of answering her, Tate went to the bottle of champagne and popped the top. The cork landed on the counter with a thump. "Garth bought the best," Tate noticed.

Because she was feeling nervous, she needed something to do. Taking two dishes from the cupboard, she cut them each a slice of white cake with coconut icing. "He seems like a good friend."

"He was a couple of years ahead of me in high school, but we were friends anyway. When he and Sandy came back to Clear Springs last year and he opened up his practice, we got reacquainted."

After Tate handed her a glass of champagne, she offered him a plate of cake. Aware of each other and the vows they'd made tonight, they sat at the table and ate in silence until Tate informed her, "I made another appointment with the lawyer tomorrow at one. The boys are in school and we can take Marie."

At the beginning of the week, when they'd seen the lawyer to finalize the prenuptial agreement, they had taken Marie along. "If I bring her bottle and a couple of toys again, she'll be fine."

"We'll probably have to answer lots of questions. Just thought I'd warn you. He'll need some background."

"I know." Finished with her plate and seeing that Tate was finished with his, she took the dishes to the sink, rinsed them and was just going to load them in the dishwasher when she dropped one of them.

Picking it up from the floor, she said, "I'm glad it didn't break."

After he rose from his chair, Tate came over to her, took it from her hands, placed it in the dishwasher and closed the machine's door. Then he faced her. "There's nothing for you to be nervous about."

"I'm not—"

He took her hand in his. "Yes, you are. You're trembling. This is going to be okay, Anita. I'm not going to rush you into anything you don't want, tonight or any time."

She couldn't help but breathe a sigh of relief, and he heard it. Still holding her hand, he suggested, "I'll walk you to your room."

All the emotions inside Anita were tumbling around, and she couldn't seem to settle them down long enough to get a good look at them. Just Tate's fingers on hers excited her. Just the thought of going to bed with him was thrilling. Yet before that happened, they needed some kind of understanding—some kind of sharing of feelings, some kind of bonding that just hadn't happened yet.

At the sitting room door, he took her face into his hands, tipped her chin up and kissed her. It was slow and sweet and sensual.

Before she had time to respond, he stopped it and stepped away. "I'll see you in the morning," he said in a low voice.

"In the morning," she breathed, and then slipped inside the door.

When she closed it, her heart was racing. Loving Tate Pardell was going to shake her world.

Each day that went by frustrated Tate more. He wanted Anita in an elemental way that was turning his stomach upside down and his brains to mush. He found himself thinking about her when he should be thinking about work. Over the weekend, he'd supervised the move of the boys into a bigger room at his end of the house and Marie into the one next to that. He'd wanted to move Anita into his bedroom, but instead, she'd hung her meager wardrobe in the third guest bedroom.

At least she was closer.

Yet not close enough.

Since the boys had full run of the house now, they were as happy as could be. In the evenings, Tate became part of their bedtime ritual and made an attempt to cut off his workday at a decent time so they could have supper as a family. The family part of everything was working out just fine. The husband and wife part...

On top of everything else, they hadn't heard a word from the Suttons' lawyer, although Tate's lawyer had informed him of Anita's marriage. That was making both him and Anita edgy.

As he helped tuck Marie in for the night, Anita's vanilla scent made him even more aware of his desire for her as he breathed it in. When he stepped close to the crib, no longer in Anita's bedroom but in a room of its own, he could hear his pulse pounding in his ears.

Running his hand down Marie's fine, curly hair, he said, "She's going to be walking soon. Did you notice how she walked all the way around the coffee table tonight while she held on?"

"I noticed. She's been doing more of that—pulling herself up and using the furniture to get from one piece to the next."

"You know, once she walks, it won't be long until she runs."

Anita laughed. "With a toddler around, I don't have to worry about joining a gym."

"Is that something you've been thinking about doing?" He couldn't keep his gaze from passing down her trim figure in her T-shirt and jeans.

"It was on my wish list once. Not so much joining a gym as just having the time to exercise."

"If you want to join the gym in town, go ahead and get a membership."

"No. It's expensive and—"

"Anita, I can afford it." When they'd signed the prenuptial agreement, Anita had said he'd been more than generous.

"Maybe *you* can. But I still don't know how much I'd use the membership, and I don't want to be wasteful. Instead, maybe I could just get an exercise bike."

"You know what we could do? We could set up one of the bedrooms in the housekeeper's quarters as an exercise room."

"That'd be great. Do you think you'd use it, too?"

"I'd make time. Maybe we could do it together." The thought of her in one of those stretchy little outfits...

He could see she was thinking about him working out, too. Her cheeks flushed and her breath came faster. Maybe tonight, if they hurried up and put the boys to bed, he'd give into temptation, kiss her long and hard and see where it led.

As if he'd conjured them up, the twins ran past Marie's room, laughing and giggling.

"I wonder what they've been up to," Anita said, worrying her lip. "They were awfully quiet while we were putting Marie to bed."

"They were probably watching TV again. They look at it as if it's a movie screen."

"They've only been to the movies a couple of times. It's a novelty for them." She checked her watch. "I'll round them up."

A beep-beep and a buzzing sound came from Tate's office down the hall.

"Is that the fax machine?" she asked.

"Sure is. I'm expecting some specs on a house I'm

going to build. I'll go pick them up and then read the boys a story."

Still thinking about Anita sliding between his sheets with him, Tate went to his office. The fax lay in its tray. He was about to pick up the paper when something on his desk made him take a second look. Before supper, he'd been studying preliminary sketches of a new model home. Now, he realized, those sketches had been colored in, over and around. The architect's preliminary drawings were absolutely ruined!

"Corey! Jared!" he bellowed before even stopping to think about it.

He didn't wait for them to make an appearance in his office. Striding furiously down the hall, he stopped at the bathroom, where they were both brushing their teeth. Their eyes were huge.

"What were you doing in my office?"

"After you and Mom got married, you said we could go in the rest of the house," Corey explained, his toothbrush dripping toothpaste onto the floor.

Tate stared down at it and felt the frustration rise up in him. He wanted to be more than "Tate" to these boys. "I didn't say you could go into my office, and I *never* said that you could touch anything in there. You ruined a week's worth of work by my architect."

"Tate," Anita broke in.

"Stay out of this, Anita. Your boys have to understand that what they did was wrong. They have to respect other people's property."

Corey and Jared were perfectly still and silent. Tate

saw tears well up in Corey's eyes as he turned and ran to his room. Jared followed his brother.

After a troubled glance at Tate, Anita headed for the boys' room, too. But he stopped her. "Wait."

Her eyes were sad. "I know they did wrong. I'll make sure they do chores for the next year to pay you back. But I need to talk to them. I don't want them to be scared of you."

Scared of him?

What had he done? Why had he reacted so strongly? Because his life had spun out of control and he couldn't seem to get a handle on it yet?

Lowering his voice, he admitted, "I don't want them to be scared of me, either. That's why *I've* got to talk to them."

To his chagrin, he saw that she wasn't sure she could trust him to do that. She didn't trust him to make her boys' well-being as important to him as it was to her. He had to show her that he could be a father to these boys—and a good one. "Give me a chance, Anita."

When she finally nodded, he hurried down the hall to the twins' room.

Corey was on his bed, hugging the old stuffed dog he slept with. Beside the bed on the floor, Jared ran a truck over the carpet.

Unsure where to begin, Tate sat down on the bed beside Corey and put his hand on the boy's shoulder.

When Corey flinched, his fear tore at Tate's heart.

"Hey, boys," he said in a gentle voice. "I want to talk about what happened."

"I'm sorry I colored on your papers," Corey mumbled, looking down at his dog.

"It was just you?" Tate asked.

"I colored one corner," Jared said from down on the floor, not looking up.

"I want you to understand—those papers weren't just something an architect does for fun. It's his job. I have to study them closely to know the best way to build a house. It takes a long time for the architect to draw them, and I pay him for doing that. So when you colored on them, you messed up his work and mine."

Corey's chin trembled, so Tate quickly hurried on. "But I don't think you meant to ruin our work, did you?"

Both boys looked up at him now and shook their heads. "We just thought it would be fun to color 'em in. We thought you might like it even," Corey explained.

Tate didn't know if he could ever learn to think like a five-year-old, but he might have to try. "Okay. But let's put it this way. If it's something you don't normally color on, you have to ask first, and it really would be best if you stay out of my office."

"Like we stay away from Mom's computer?" Jared asked.

"Yeah, exactly like that." He patted the bed and said, "Come up here and sit, Jared."

When Jared and Corey were facing him, he told them, "I've never been a dad before, so I'm going to have to learn how to do this day by day. I'm probably going to make mistakes. But I want to be your father, and I want you as my sons. How does that sound to you?"

"We need a dad," Jared said seriously. "Are you gonna punish us for what we did?"

"That's a sticky one. You didn't mean any harm, but you caused some damage. So how about if you boys help me muck out the barn on Saturday and we'll call it even."

Out of the corner of his eye, Tate could see Anita standing in the doorway, and he wondered how long she'd been there. But then he saw the tender look of admiration and respect in her green eyes for him.

Right now, that meant more to him than having her in his bed.

Chapter Eight

On Thursday evening, Tate came home, eager to see Anita's reaction to his surprise. Last night, after the kids were in bed, he'd gone to his room without making a pass. He'd decided he had to actively court his wife. Unsure of the best way to do that, he chose to start with what most women liked: clothes. After a few phone calls early that morning, he discovered a store in Tyler that used a personal shopper. After he'd gotten the woman on the line, the rest had been easy. By offering an extra bonus to the driver, the clothes should have been delivered that afternoon.

But when he found Anita in the living room with the boxes open and clothes spread around—Marie sitting on the floor, playing with plastic containers, and the boys running a fire engine with sound effects across the wide room—her expression wasn't happy but troubled.

"Don't they fit?" he asked, thinking maybe the problem was that he had misjudged her size.

"They'll fit, but I can't accept them," she said in a low voice. Her gaze fell on a sexy ice-blue nightgown and robe set tumbling out of the box on the hassock.

Damn! If she thought this was simply a bribe to get her into bed...

In a near-whisper that he had to get very close to hear, she declared, "All my life, I've made my own way. If you start dressing me, along with giving us food and shelter and helping me keep my kids, I don't know if I can hold on to my self-respect."

Day by day, he was beginning to believe that Anita was genuine, that she didn't have ulterior motives, that she hadn't married him to drain his bank account. If she was an actress, she was a damn good one and he deserved to be fooled. The glistening in her eyes now told him she meant every word.

As always, he couldn't keep from touching her and brushing her glossy, curly hair behind her ear. "As your husband, I want to provide for you. You spend so much time taking care of me and my house. Don't you see I want to give something back to you? Can't you accept the clothes as a present from me?"

"I feel a bit like Cinderella," she said with a small smile. This time, her gaze fell on an emerald-green gown with a beaded bodice carefully folded in a box on the sofa. "All I need is a ball."

"Clear Springs is a little small for a ball. But how about enjoying a good band and dinner-dance at the country club this weekend? The women dress snazzy, and the men pull out their best suits. If Inez can babysit, we'll have the whole night to ourselves, the way a husband and wife should sometimes."

Each day, he was going to bring something home for her: candy, flowers, some kind of trinket. Soon, she'd get the message that he truly wanted her to be his wife.

"A night with you sounds wonderful," she admitted a bit breathlessly.

If she was as excited about the prospect as he was, he was making progress. Just so she was clear on what he wanted, he gave her another hint. "If all those clothes won't fit in your closet, you can hang them in mine."

The pulse at her throat beat faster, her lips parted slightly and he wanted to sweep her into his arms and take her into his bed right now. But patience usually paid off.

Unexpectedly, she went up on her tiptoes and kissed him on the cheek. "Thank you, Tate. I owe you so much."

That kiss was affectionate and tender and as arousing as any that had happened before. He appreciated her thanks, but he didn't want it. He wanted *her.*

On Saturday night, maybe he'd get his wish.

Tate was in the great room the following evening, encouraging Marie to walk while the twins watched TV, the red roses he'd brought home for Anita arranged in a vase on a side table.

When the doorbell rang, Anita threw down her dish towel, called "I'll get it" and went to the foyer. When she opened the door, she was stunned to see the couple who stood there—Warren and Ruth Sutton.

"I know you're wondering why we're here," Warren

was quick to explain, "but our lawyer informed us about your marriage and we wanted to make sure for ourselves that you *had* gotten married."

No matter what, Anita told herself, she had to be polite. She couldn't give these people any more reason to resent her.

"Why don't you come in," she invited. "We were about to have supper. Would you like to join us?"

Before they could answer, Tate was by her side, holding Marie in his arms.

After she introduced him to the couple, he said in a friendly way, "Anita's told me about you. I can understand that grandparents would want to know their grandkids."

Nervously switching her purse from one hand to the other, Ruth assured him, "Yes, we do. We're thinking about dropping the custody suit. We would like to stay in Clear Springs for the weekend and spend some time with Corey, Jared and Marie, if you're open to that."

Anita exchanged a look with Tate and then responded. "We're open to that."

"Can you suggest a good motel?" Ruth asked.

After a long, silent moment, Tate offered, "Why don't you stay here with us? That'll give us all a chance to get to know each other better."

Shell-shocked by Tate's offer, Anita wondered if he was out of his mind.

The Suttons looked surprised by his invitation, and Anita realized almost at once that he'd *meant* to catch them off guard. He wanted to quell their doubts, and the invitation might do just that. Maybe they wouldn't accept—

"Could you give my wife and me a minute to discuss this?" Warren asked.

"No problem," Tate said as he took Anita's arm and tugged her toward the kitchen.

Once inside, Anita turned to him. "What are you doing? We don't want them in the house all weekend!" She kept her voice low, but it was filled with all the anxiety she was feeling.

"The best way to get them on our side is to show them we *are* a family. If we send them to a motel, they might think we have something to hide. They can stay in the guest room, but you're going to have to move in with me tonight."

She studied him to see if that was the real reason he had suggested this.

"What?" he asked, all innocent-looking.

"One of us is going to have to sleep somewhere other than the bed."

With a sigh, he said, "I have a recliner in there. I can sleep on it."

She didn't know why she was resisting the pull between them with so much energy. Maybe because she was simply terrified to give herself to him completely. Once they made love, there was no turning back.

Suddenly, she remembered something. "I'd better get the cosmetics out of my bathroom and put them in yours, as well as pick up anything else that's lying around. Do you have any spare drawers?"

He grinned then asked, "How many do you need?"

"Two."

"No problem," he assured her. "I have two empty ones in my chest."

"Because they *are* going to accept your offer. They're going to want to know everything there is to know about us."

Slowly, in a husky voice, he said, "We don't have anything to hide, Anita."

"We don't have a real marriage yet," she returned, tears coming to her eyes because she realized she *wanted* a real marriage, but not merely because that was the convenient road to take.

"But soon we will." He caressed her cheek. "Go move your toothbrush next to mine. I'll keep them occupied."

Marie squiggled and squirmed in his arms. "Or Marie will," he added with a wink.

As Anita had concluded, Ruth and Warren Sutton decided to accept their offer. After an evening filled with the kids' laughter, Marie's toddling from chair to chair finally letting Ruth pick her up, Anita showed the Suttons to the guest room, exhausted.

After a last check on the boys and Marie to make sure they were sleeping, she finally entered Tate's bedroom, feeling like a stranger there.

"Uh-oh," she muttered. "I forgot about my clothes in the guest room closet."

"Maybe Ruth won't snoop."

"What are the chances of that? How am I going to explain?"

Not seeming bothered at all by the situation, Tate gave a shrug. "That's easy. I bought you a new wardrobe and it's in here. You can just tell her that. We're okay, Anita. Stop worrying."

But she *was* worrying. Not only about the Suttons and her new wardrobe but also about that sexy new nightgown Tate had bought her. She had no choice but to wear it tonight.

Then she remembered the long T-shirt he'd included with a longhorn steer imprinted on the cotton. She'd put that on.

Along with sweaters, slacks and dresses, the personal shopper Tate had consulted had included panties and bras in gossamer fabrics. All of them were in the master suite. She hadn't worn any of them yet. This morning, she'd dragged on her old clothes out of habit.

Now she went to the chest, ignored the silk nightie and pulled out the T-shirt.

"If you want to use the bathroom first, go ahead," he offered as he sat in the recliner and held a horse magazine in his hands, acting as if she slept there every night. He seemed as if nothing about this predicament was unusual.

"Don't you feel awkward?" she asked him. "Don't you mind that the Suttons are asking personal questions and poking into our lives? Or that we're still feeling our way and don't know if this marriage is going to take or not?"

She had lowered her voice on that last one, even though the boys' room and Marie's were between the master suite and the guest bedroom.

With resolve, Tate lowered the footrest on the recliner, stood and ambled over to her. "When I built this house, I wasn't sure why I built something so big.

Maybe because I had the money to do it. Maybe because I'd always wanted a place with horses. At least, those were the things I told myself. But deep down, I guess I dreamed of having a family. We're taking care of the kids and living in this house together, and we're legally married. Those people will see we're building something here, so stop worrying so much."

Worrying was a trait she'd developed when she was a child and knew they couldn't pay the rent. It was an old habit that she couldn't just let go of because Tate suggested it. "I'll stop worrying when they're gone and I know they're not still trying to fight me for my kids. I won't be long in the bathroom," she murmured as she slipped away from him, still battling to stand on her own two feet, still struggling to trust Tate when giving her trust had hurt her unbearably before.

When Anita came out of the bathroom, Tate was removing pajama bottoms from a drawer. "I never wear these," he said, "but tonight I will. Looks like that T-shirt fits you just like it should."

To her dismay, the cotton clung to her curves and stopped a few inches above her knees. The negligee set couldn't have been much more revealing. Scurrying to the bed, she slipped under the covers.

With a small smile tilting the corners of his lips, Tate disappeared into the bathroom.

After he emerged, he was wearing the plaid pajama bottoms, the drawstring tied loosely at his navel. But he wore no shirt, and she couldn't seem to unglue her eyes from his chest. He was magnificently built. As he came over to the bed, she thought he might kiss her or do something that would lead them into each other's arms. But he didn't. He simply picked up the coverlet folded at the foot of the bed and took it to the recliner, where he settled himself as if it didn't bother him at all not to be sleeping in his bed or that *she* was sleeping in his bed.

"Can you get the light?" he asked in a slightly perfunctory voice as he pulled the cover midchest and reclined as far back as the chair would take him.

Oh, she could get the light, all right. At least that way, she could stop staring at him. The only problem was, every detail of his body was branded into her memory. At least every detail of the parts she'd seen. When she thought about the parts she *hadn't* seen…

She shivered, excited yet scared…scared that if she gave her heart away, it was going to get broken.

When Anita awoke, the bedroom was still black and she realized what had summoned her from sleep—the squeaks and crunches from Tate's recliner as he tried to get comfortable.

It only took her a moment of hesitation before she asked, "Tate?"

"What?" His voice was tempered.

"There's no reason why you can't sleep in this bed with me. We're both adults."

The recliner squeaked again. "Are you sure about that? It's a king-size bed and all, but I don't want you to be uncomfortable with the idea."

"I trust you," she said simply and knew she did—at least where this was concerned. Tate would never force her into anything she didn't want.

A few beats of silence ticked by. Then Tate lowered the footrest on his recliner and crossed over to the other side of the bed. He didn't say a word—just slid in and turned away from her. A few minutes later, she heard his deep, heavy breathing and knew he was asleep. She didn't know how *she* was going to sleep with his bare back merely a foot away!

Sometime in the early hours of the morning, she and Tate came together. She didn't know how it happened, but in the morning, his arms were around her, her cheek against his chest, and they were curled intimately together. She awoke first and lay perfectly still, not knowing what to do. She'd had a dream where he'd taken her in his arms…

Apparently it hadn't been a dream.

When she untucked her hand from underneath him, he came awake. "What the heck?"

"I guess we were cold," she murmured, pulling away from him.

He quickly let her go. "Yeah, I guess we must have been. I've got to tend to the horses," he said, sliding his legs over the bed. "The Suttons probably won't be up for another hour or so. I should be able to help you with the kids and breakfast, if you need it."

She didn't know if she needed it, but she wanted it. Too much.

"I'll be able to handle everything. Don't worry."

At the edge of the bed, he glanced at her over his shoulder. "You know, it's okay to put your pride and independence aside once in a while."

"I've set my pride and independence aside a lot with

you. I don't know if I like the idea of being protected and rescued, and you've done both."

"You don't believe in the fairy tale?"

"I've had reason not to. Besides, in those fairy tales, the women were too passive. I want to believe I control my own destiny."

He shook his head. "You are one tough lady."

"You aren't one tough man?" she tossed back.

"Okay," he sighed, "it's a draw. Go back to sleep and I'll get out of your hair."

Go back to sleep—after being curled in his arms...after having that conversation...after wishing things were different between them. Sure, she wanted the dreams and the future that went with a fairy tale. But love and commitment had to be part of that.

After Tate left the room, she showered and dressed. Going down the hall to Marie's room, she was about to push open the door when Ruth came out of the guest bedroom and saw her. Anita automatically smiled, bracing herself for whatever came next.

"I have a question for you," Ruth said brightly, "before you wake up that beautiful little girl."

"She might be awake already."

"This will only take a minute. Not that I was snooping or anything, but when I opened the closet, I found your clothes in it. I thought that was kind of odd that you're living in this big house and still have clothes in the guest room closet."

Grateful she'd remembered to sweep her cosmetics from the sink and anything personal from the medicine cabinet, as well as her clothes from the dresser drawers, she told herself to stay calm. "It's not so odd, really. Tate bought me a new wardrobe after we were married." She flitted her hand against the beautiful royal-blue, raw-silk sweater and slacks that she was wearing this morning. "This is one of the outfits. He found a personal shopper to help him and she did a wonderful job, don't you think?"

Ruth had almost been gleeful when she'd asked the question, as if she'd caught Anita in something she shouldn't have. Now she just looked totally defeated. "Yes, she did do a wonderful job. And Tate must be a very thoughtful man to do that for you. Tell me something. Did you marry him for his money as well as to protect your right to your children?"

Anita's cheeks blazed as a bunch of turbulent emotions swirled inside of her. Finally, the answer came easily. "I don't care what you and your husband think, but I love Tate Pardell, and that's why I married him."

All of a sudden, Ruth's righteousness slipped from her shoulders. "You really mean that, don't you?"

"Yes, I do. And my children are growing to love him, too."

"In a way they never loved Larry?" Ruth guessed.

"Your son was…"

When she paused, Ruth jumped in. "My son was selfish. I know that. He couldn't see beyond what he wanted from moment to moment. That's why he was a handful. That's why he got into trouble. He never seemed to look ahead to the consequences. But he was still my son, and I loved him. I wanted to search for him the whole time he was gone, but Warren said we had to remain firm. He believed that when Larry made a success of his life, he'd contact us or come home, and he really didn't want to hear from Larry otherwise. It just about broke my heart. Now, since we learned about Larry's death, Warren is a different man. He actually broke down and cried when we heard. I've never seen him cry as long as we've been married."

"I'm so sorry this turned out the way it did," Anita said, meaning it.

Ruth let out a huge breath. "I think Warren and I have handled this all wrong. We just felt so guilty about Larry, we wanted to give Corey, Jared and Marie absolutely everything we can."

"I know you do. But most important of all is your time, love and attention. I know that's going to be hard with you in Houston and us living here. But we can make it happen. I know how important you can be to the children. I won't try to cut you out of our lives...."

"Unless we do you harm. I understand that."

With an idea forming, Anita smiled. "Tate and I were supposed to go to a dinner-dance tonight at the country club. After you spend the day with the kids, do you think you and Warren would like to go? We can change our plans and stay home, but if you'd like, I'm sure Tate can arrange for two more tickets. It will give us all a chance to get to know each other better."

"I'll talk to Warren about it. But in the meantime, can I help you get Marie up?"

Feeling happy inside, Anita knew she could be generous to this couple who wanted grandchildren to love. "Sure. Maybe she'll even let you dress her."

Ruth's face suddenly filled with joy and Anita felt good that she could give her that. If she and the Suttons could become friends rather than adversaries, the children would be better off.

With the threat of the Suttons taking custody gone, would Tate really want to adopt Corey, Jared and Marie and become a real father?

Only time would tell.

That night, when Tate took Anita into his arms on the country club's dance floor, he felt like a teenager with hormones he didn't know how to control. Apparently, last night in his sleep, he'd enfolded Anita in his arms. When he'd awakened, surprised and fully aroused, he'd gotten out of that bedroom fast. He'd never expected that patience would kill him, but he was beginning to think it would. Now admiring his wife in a beautiful new gown—her shoulders bare, her hair a mound of curls on top of her head—he drew her closer, unsure he could handle another night in the same bed with her without a steel divider between them.

"You look beautiful," he murmured into her ear.

When she turned her face toward his, her lips almost grazed his jaw. "You look pretty good yourself."

He'd worn the suit he'd used for their wedding.

Before he kissed Anita and dragged her out on the terrace to make love to her, he asked, "How'd it go with Ruth this afternoon?" That afternoon, Ruth and Anita had gone shopping and Ruth had found a dress appropriate for the occasion, too.

Anita glanced over at Ruth and Warren Sutton, who were also dancing. "She's hurting. She has been for years, ever since Larry left them. But I think the children are helping. How about you and Warren? Did you get a chance to talk while you kept the twins and Marie occupied?"

"A little. He didn't say too much. Just that he knew he was lax with Larry when he was growing up. He thinks we're doing a good job with the kids."

"I hope so," she breathed. Her gaze going to the Suttons again, she commented, "Do you think Warren looks all right tonight? His complexion is a little gray."

"His spirits seemed good enough. I saw him taking some of that stomach medication this afternoon. Being a banker and all, maybe he has an ulcer."

"Houston is far away," she said with a sigh. "If we want to visit them, what will you do about the horses? If they're a problem, I could always drive down myself for a weekend."

"The horses won't be a problem," he responded gruffly, wondering if she'd rather go alone. "I have enough people who can come in and take care of them." Then he had to put his concern into words. "Maybe you'd rather go yourself. After all, Corey, Jared and Marie were Larry's kids, not mine."

Her gaze on his, she answered, "I'd like you to come along. I was just making sure you wanted to."

"I know you put them first, and I'm going to do that, too."

Her smile was beaming as she laid her head against his shoulder and he wrapped his arms around her. Dancing could be the next best thing to making love.

* * *

After they got home that evening, Anita bid the Suttons good-night as Tate drove Inez home. She moved around the bedroom, hanging up a pair of Tate's jeans he'd left over a chair, noticing her new wardrobe on one side of the walk-in closet while his clothes hung on the other side. They were melding their lives together. Tonight, as she'd danced in his arms, she'd been almost dizzy with desire for him.

So why was she holding back?

Because she was afraid to take the leap. Because she'd been hurt before. Because she didn't want to be betrayed again.

But could she ever have the real marriage she wanted without sharing the one act that could unite them into man and wife?

Tate was obviously a patient man, but she didn't know how long he could remain patient. She didn't know how long it would be until resentment crept in.

Tonight, she had to take the biggest risk of her life.

Although she'd showered earlier in the evening, she quickly did so again and donned the pretty blue negligee set he'd bought her. It skimmed her skin like gossamer. She was belting the robe when the bedroom door opened and Tate came inside. When he saw her, he stood stock still.

"I want to make our marriage a real one," she said in a breathless voice. "Do you?"

She waited, her heart racing so fast she could hardly breathe....

Chapter Nine

Tate was absolutely speechless. Then he didn't know what to do, which was ludicrous. He always knew what to do with a woman.

But this was Anita, and he'd never been married before.

"Are you sure?" He couldn't believe he wasn't just grabbing her and throwing her on the bed. But something was making him hesitate. Something was making him take his time.

"I'm sure."

Her words lit so many fires inside of him, he didn't know if he'd ever get them all under control again.

As he walked toward her, he braced himself against feeling too much. After all, she could turn tail and run.

But she didn't. She just stood there, looking at him with those incredible green eyes.

He shrugged out of his suit coat and tossed it onto a

chair, then loosened his bolo tie and threw it on the dresser, where it landed with a plunk. Next, he opened a few top buttons of his shirt. She didn't move or say anything.

"What prompted this, Anita?" he asked, attempting to stay logical and trying to keep his voice even.

"Sleeping with you last night and waking up with you this morning. If you want our marriage to be more than words on paper, this is part of it."

This was certainly part of it, a part he'd wanted since he'd set eyes on her. However, now it was about to become real, with consequences, and he couldn't just throw caution to the wind.

"If I'm wrong and you don't want me…" she said, with her voice catching.

"I want you." As gritty as the words were, they were true. A few more steps and he stood before her, towering over her. "You've been in my dreams since the day I interviewed you," he confided.

"You've been in mine, too."

She obviously wasn't going to make the first move—the first physical move. She was leaving that up to him. He liked that. He liked a woman who was a little shy, who wasn't all sure of herself.

When his hands went to her shoulders, he could feel her tremble. "Are you scared?" he asked, not expecting that.

Giving him a small smile, she responded, "Excited. Scared. Unsure. I've only ever been with Larry. And I know you've probably been…"

"Just so you know, I'm careful. I've never put myself at risk. And I got tested last year." This wasn't the time to think about having more kids, either. He'd be careful tonight, too.

When his hands slowly slid up her neck and his thumbs caressed her cheek, holding back became a thing of the past. His lips sealed to hers. His tongue slid into her mouth and coherent thought had no place in the midst of his desire. Seconds later, his hands were on the satiny tie to her robe. Hers were unbuttoning the rest of his shirt. Quicker than he could say his name, he had her naked. Looking at her fueled his arousal, and he knew he had to get his boots off fast.

Scooping her into his arms, he carried her to the bed and laid her down, then made quick work of the rest of his clothes. Before he slid into bed, though, he reached into the nightstand, pulled out a few packets and laid them by the alarm clock.

She was watching him intently, and something passed across her face when she saw the condoms. Did she want kids to tie them together more securely? To make sure he had a financial responsibility toward her? They hadn't spelled out anything about their offspring in the prenuptial.

But he didn't stop to analyze any more of it. He couldn't. He was on fire with need for her. Tonight, he intended to satisfy that need.

They came together in the middle of the big bed, just as they had last night. But there were no thoughts of sleep as he reached for her, ran his large hands down her satiny skin, caressed her breasts in a way that made her moan and kissed her with a ferocity he didn't know he possessed.

She was more than ready when he entered her. His

heart practically stopped with the sensation of it, then his breath came raggedly.

With monumental effort, he held on to his control until she called his name. But then the expression on her face, the flush on her cheeks, her hands on his body pushed him over the edge. Even so, he was aware that she climaxed again, and he felt proud and satisfied about that as he let the ecstasy of joining overtake him and turn his world upside down.

Anita was awake the following morning when Tate slid out of bed. He hadn't held her through the night as he had the night before. After the first time, they'd dozed awhile and then made love all over again. At least, *she* had made love. She wasn't sure about Tate. He'd made her body sing, and in return, she'd given him pleasures she hadn't given a man before. But afterward, no tender words had come from him—no gentle, lingering caresses. Maybe she hadn't pleased him at all. Maybe he'd been disappointed.

As she looked up at him this morning and saw the grave expression on his face, she wondered if he was sorry he'd jumped into this whole situation.

"I've let chores mount up in the barn," he said. "I'll come back in for breakfast to say goodbye to Ruth and Warren. But the rest of the day, I've got to catch up on tack cleaning, mucking out the stalls and building cupboards for gear."

"You don't have someone who can do that for you?" she asked lightly, trying to fish out his real reason for not wanting to spend time with her and the kids.

He gave her an odd look. "Some things I like to do myself. I'll be back in an hour or so."

As the bedroom door closed, tears came to Anita's eyes. This wasn't at all what she'd expected. She'd expected they'd feel closer, not farther apart. She'd expected maybe to tell Tate how much she cared for him, and maybe he'd admit some of his feelings for her.

"Grow up," she told herself sternly as she got out of bed. "You know how men are. They take what they want and then they bail out."

Nevertheless, she had thought Tate was different. Maybe *she* was the problem. Maybe she wasn't doing something right. After all, Larry had strayed early in their marriage and kept doing so. Obviously, there must have been a reason.

Wiping away a few tears, she reminded herself she and Tate had both been under a lot of stress lately and he'd seen a lot of changes in his life—kids, marriage and in-laws. She needed to give them both a break.

After she showered and dressed, she went to the mirror to brush her hair. It seemed funny having her possessions interspersed with Tate's. When she picked up her brush, she saw his keys and wallet lying on a wooden valet. Then she spotted the money clip holding a wad of bills. It wasn't the money that caught her attention, though.

There was an engraving on the clip, and curiosity got the better of her. Picking it up, she read the inscription—All My Love, Donna.

Who was Donna? What had she meant to Tate? If she was a former girlfriend, why would he have kept the money clip? Did he still have feelings for her? Wasn't their relationship over?

Tate had slowly let his guard down with Anita, and last night she had felt a closeness between them. Then this morning, he'd been remote and his walls had been back—firmly in place. If she asked him about the money clip, what would happen?

Wasn't there enough tension between them? Even if the money clip was from a former girlfriend, wasn't the past in the past? They seemed to have enough trouble dealing with the present.

Setting down the clip, she prayed for the day when Tate could share his innermost thoughts with her. She prayed for the day when she wouldn't be afraid to be vulnerable to him.

It was midweek when Ruth Sutton called Anita. "I hope you don't mind me checking in."

Normally, Anita wouldn't mind at all. But today, Marie was crying. She had been fussing since morning and wouldn't take a bottle. Her nose was running a little and Anita was worried. She was also frazzled. She hadn't been sleeping well. Since the weekend, Tate had worked long hours, coming home after she was asleep. Or, at least, he thought she was asleep. This morning, he'd left a note that he was leaving tomorrow for a business trip to Dallas. She didn't even know how long he'd be gone!

"I don't mind you checking in, but I don't know if Marie's going to cooperate. She has the sniffles. She got me up around six this morning and still won't settle down for a nap."

"Maybe she's teething."

New teeth were constantly popping through, and she knew Ruth could be right. "Maybe. She's just not usually this cranky."

"Well, I won't keep you. I just wondered if we could set up a visit in a couple of weeks. Maybe you could come down here. We have plenty of room. Warren just doesn't seem like himself since we got back. I think he's missing your brood."

"Is he feeling okay?"

"He's just dealing with that indigestion of his. Do you think Tate can get away for a weekend?"

The way Tate had been acting, she was afraid to ask. But she wouldn't make the same mistakes in this marriage she'd made in her last one. They had a few things to talk about, and maybe tonight was the night— before he left for the business trip to Dallas tomorrow. She couldn't let issues slide anymore.

"I'll talk to him when he gets home. He's been working long hours."

"See if you can fit it in."

Marie began wailing again.

Above the ruckus, Ruth practically shouted over the phone, "We can always have a driver bring you down."

"That won't be necessary. As soon as I talk to Tate, I'll give you a call back, okay?"

"That'll be fine. You can reach me any time on my cell phone. Did I give you that number?"

Anita had tucked the slip of paper into her purse. "Yes, I have it."

"Give the children a kiss for me."

"I will," Anita assured her, trying to hold the phone while she jiggled Marie, trying not to make Ruth feel as if she was brushing her off.

During the next hour, Marie wouldn't stop crying. Anita changed her, rocked her and encouraged her to sip from her cup. She walked her through the living room, put on some music, lay her against her shoulder and patted her back.

"Oh, baby. I don't know what to do for you." Just as she said the words, Marie spit up the milk Anita had managed to get her to drink.

Amid Marie's cries, Anita realized she had to go to the bus stop for the boys. She bundled up her fussing baby and took her out to her car seat.

Fortunately, the boys' bus was on time. They ran to the car and climbed inside, but backed up when they heard their sister squealing.

"What's wrong with her?" Jared asked.

"I don't know. I might have to take her to the doctor."

The twins could see she was worried, but that didn't stop them from poking and picking on each other on the short ride to the house. They'd been cooped up in a classroom all day, and she knew they needed to let off steam, too.

Still, her crying baby girl was taking most of Anita's attention.

"Can we play ball in the yard?" Corey asked.

The backyard was fenced in and she could easily see them from the kitchen window. "All right. But not for too long. I want you to get cleaned up for supper."

Red-faced now, Marie waved her arms as tears ran

down her little cheeks. Corey and Jared ran to the garage for the baseball bat and mitts, then hurried out back. A few minutes later, Anita saw Corey pitch the ball to Jared.

Satisfied they'd be there for a few minutes, she found the ear thermometer in Marie's room and took her temperature. It was 101 degrees. She usually took the kids to a clinic in town. Going back to the kitchen, holding Marie close to her, she tried to make a call to the nurse there, but the line was busy. Even though she hit Redial several times, the call didn't go through. It was the end of the day. She'd just have to keep trying. In the meantime, though, she had to cool Marie down. She'd been lucky. Her baby hadn't been sick before this, but that also meant she didn't have any medicine on hand.

Taking Marie to the bathroom, she began to fill the baby tub with tepid water.

Tate drove his truck around the back of the house instead of pulling into the garage, knowing he was avoiding going inside. Since he'd made love to Anita, he'd been trying to get things straight in his head. Sensations he'd never felt before had overwhelmed him when they'd come together. She'd given him more pleasure than any woman ever had. And he'd taken more pleasure than he could ever remember taking.

But it hadn't been all about pleasure, and that was the problem. He didn't like the idea of a woman shaking him up, and Anita had done that from the get-go. He'd thought the prenuptial agreement would prevent a Donna-like occurrence from happening again, but he still wasn't so sure. He and Anita had known each other less than two months. How could any man know a woman in that amount of time?

He wanted to just trust her but he still had his doubts....

Anita had taken such delight in her new wardrobe yet at first hadn't wanted to accept it. Had that simply been a ploy to convince him she was on the up-and-up?

She'd slipped into his lifestyle so easily. On Saturday at the country club, she'd fit right in, as if she'd been practicing all her life. He'd told himself it was her genuine friendliness, not any type of manipulation, that made people like her. She'd even handled her in-laws tactfully and won them over.

Still, he'd remembered her comment when he'd said he was going to build some cupboards. *You don't have someone who can do that for you*? Had she just been practical? Or was she coming to expect that money bought privileges and made things a hell of a lot easier?

Then there had been that night when she'd stood before him in her nightgown and robe, looking like every man's fantasy. Why the sudden turnaround?

He'd thought time would give him answers, but time seemed to be complicating the situation even more. And tomorrow he had to go to Dallas on business for a day or two.

When he rounded the bend to the barn, he stomped on the brakes, not believing what he saw. Corey and Jared weren't standing outside the corral, looking in on the horses. Instead, Corey was on the top rung of the fence, and as Tate watched, he dropped into the corral. Jared climbed up and joined his twin on the other side as Corey pulled long grass from around one of the fence posts and approached Comet, one of the Appaloosas.

In a streak of motion, Tate was out of the truck, clamping his Stetson tighter on his head. "Corey! Jared!" he yelled. "Get away from them."

The boys looked startled, then afraid. Pewter Lady, Tate's favorite of the horses he'd bought, saw the boys and trotted over to them at a fast clip.

Tate's heart sank into his stomach. He jumped over the fence, ran between her and the twins and caught her halter.

"Get inside the barn," he told the boys, keeping his voice controlled.

They stood frozen for a moment, and he realized that if he wasn't careful he'd have the same situation he had that day when they'd colored the plans in his office. "Go into the barn," he said in a gentler tone. "It's not safe for you to be out here. We'll talk about it when I come in."

When Tate entered the barn, the boys were standing by one of the stalls, hands in their pockets, looking dejected and fearful.

His heart still thudding madly, fear for their safety uppermost in his mind, memories of what had happened to his brother, Jeremy, plaguing him, Tate got control of the past, realized he was in the present and crouched down before them.

"Didn't I tell you never to go out with the horses alone?"

"We weren't alone," Corey piped up. "We were with each other."

Tate almost groaned in frustration at the literal translation of his order. "I think you knew what I meant. But whether you did or not, I want to make it clear. Horses aren't like dogs or cats. They're big animals. I don't think the horses I bought would hurt you on purpose, but because they're so big, because they run so fast, they *could* hurt you, even not meaning to."

"You mean one of them could trample us?" Corey asked, looking aghast, as if he'd never thought of it before.

"Their hooves are strong and heavy and hard. Just imagine what it would be like if *I* stepped on your foot. One of those horses weighs a heck of a lot more than I do."

"We want to ride and you won't let us," Jared admitted. "We just wanted to touch them and feed them. There weren't any more apples left in the bin, so we were going to try that long grass."

Standing, Tate took off his Stetson, rubbed his hand through his hair and plopped it back on his head. This past week, he hadn't been a very good dad. Now he could see why fathers had to be around...why they couldn't expect kids just to raise themselves...why they couldn't work fifteen hours a day and expect their boys to grow up with morals, respect and the ability to be dads themselves someday.

"Why isn't your mom watching you?" He found anger rising toward Anita for letting the boys roam around on their own.

"She was busy with Marie."

When he was silent for a few moments, Corey asked, "Are you going to punish us?"

"Since we had a little misunderstanding about what going into the corral alone meant, I'm not going to punish you this time. But from now on, you don't set foot near a horse till I say you can."

They both looked crestfallen.

"In exchange, when I get back from my trip, maybe we'll saddle up Pewter Lady and I'll give each of you a short ride. You can be around them more when I'm here. Got it?"

The two boys grinned at him. "Got it," they said in unison.

"Now what I want you to do is go into the house, go to your room and find something to play with for a while. I have to talk to your mom."

As the boys ran out of the barn into the house, Tate followed more slowly, disturbed by what almost happened. What had Anita been doing? Why had she let the boys anywhere near the barn?

When Tate came home from work, Anita was usually in the kitchen, making dinner. Tonight she wasn't. He found her in the bathroom, kneeling by the tub, running a cloth over Marie. Why was she giving her a bath now?

After she glanced up at him, she gazed back at her daughter. "Thanks for bringing the boys in. I had to—"

"Your boys almost got trampled by a horse."

That brought her gaze back to his again. "What do you mean? They were playing catch!"

"No, they weren't playing catch. They were in the corral. Do you know how dangerous that is? Why weren't you watching them?"

"I was watching them. I mean, as much as I could. Marie has a temperature and I can't reach the doctor—"

When he saw the tears flood his wife's eyes, Tate

realized this wasn't an ordinary situation. It wasn't like Anita not to know where those boys were every second, and he should have understood that.

Kneeling down beside her, he put his hand to Marie's brow. "She has a fever?"

"Yes, and a runny nose. I don't know if anything else is going on or not. I couldn't get through to the doctor, so I was just trying to cool her down a bit. But I have to try calling again. It's just that I seem to need five hands at once—and a second pair of eyes."

Usually composed and expertly in command of her kids, Tate had never seen Anita frazzled like this before. He couldn't keep from dropping his arm around her shoulders. "Hey, it'll be all right. I'll call Garth. He'll tell us what to do."

"I don't have insurance since Larry died. I've been paying as I go at the clinic."

"I put you and the kids on my policy after our wedding. You're covered." Tears that had welled up began to roll down her cheeks, and he wiped one of them away. "The boys are in their room playing. They'll be fine for five minutes or so. I'll call Garth and we'll go from there."

Tate had Garth's private pager number, and he used it. Fortunately, the physician was just leaving his office for the day. "I'll stop by. I'll be there in five minutes."

Anita had just finished dressing Marie in a clean terry cloth playsuit when Tate brought Garth into the bedroom. After a quick examination, he said, "I don't think this is anything to be too concerned about. She has a slight infection in one ear. I'll call in a prescription and you can pick it up at the drugstore."

Holding her baby close and rocking her back and forth, Anita said to Garth, "You don't know how much I appreciate this. I was beginning to get really worried."

"Kids can spike a fever pretty fast. You did the right thing by calling me," he said to Tate.

As Garth left the room, Tate clasped her shoulder. "I'll take the boys with me. Then you won't have to worry about them."

"Are you sure you want to do that?"

"I haven't spent enough time with them this week. We'll stop and get takeout on our way back. How about some burgers and fries?"

"That sounds good," she breathed with relief. "Tate, I'm sorry they went into the corral. Can I ask how you handled it?"

"We had a discussion. I think they understand now how worried I am about their safety. But I also told them I'd give them short rides when I get back from Dallas. I can't be unreasonable. I was only overprotective because—"

"Because?"

His eyes stayed on hers. "When I was twelve and my brother, Jeremy, was ten, we went riding. He wanted to take out a horse I knew he shouldn't ride. But he was a daredevil and so was I. We were racing and something startled his horse. He fell off, hit his head against a rock and that was that. He was gone."

Quiet now and exhausted, Marie lay against Anita's shoulder.

"Tate, I'm so sorry," Anita murmured, hurting for him.

"I still blame myself."

"You shouldn't! Accidents happen. You were twelve. A twelve-year-old doesn't have the judgment of an adult."

"A twelve-year-old doesn't know how to follow good instincts. My gut instincts told me he shouldn't take the horse out. Now I follow my gut."

And his gut instincts were telling him Anita was the real deal. If he didn't let go of the past, he would lose her. Tipping her chin up, he gave her a soft, slow kiss. "We'll be back in a little while."

As he went down to the boys' room to fetch them, he knew Marie's cold might keep them up all night. Even if it did, he'd be beside Anita. If they did manage to get some sleep, he'd be holding his wife in his arms.

Chapter Ten

It was almost four a.m. when Marie finally fell asleep, and Anita was exhausted. Tate had stayed up with her, helping her however he could. He'd even walked Marie himself several times during the night, murmuring to her. Anita had told him more than once to go to bed, but he had just given her that half smile of his and said they were in this together.

How she wanted to believe him.

She was undressing when he came into the bedroom. "Thank Garth for me when you see him for coming out tonight. I know doctors don't make house calls anymore."

"Garth is a good friend. So is Sandy. You'll have to get to know them better."

Actually, she hadn't thought much about having a social life with Tate, but now the idea of getting together with Sandy and Garth was pleasant.

As tired as she was, she couldn't help admiring Tate

as he undressed. They hadn't been in the same room together—when they were awake—intimately like this since they'd made love.

"Do you remember that I'm leaving for Dallas today?"

"I'd forgotten," she said with a sigh. Then she added truthfully, "I'll miss you."

If she'd hoped he'd say he'd miss her, he didn't.

She climbed into bed first. Then Tate slid under the covers and turned out the light. But he didn't stay away as he had since the weekend.

Rather, he turned toward her and opened his arms. "Come here. Let me hold you while you fall asleep."

As she snuggled into Tate's arms, her back against his chest, she felt his almost immediate arousal.

"It's okay," he murmured close to her ear. "Go to sleep."

She knew she could set the course for what happened next. "I'm tired, but I'm wired, too. Do you know what I mean?"

"Like you've been through a crisis and now are feeling the aftereffects of the adrenaline?" he suggested.

Turning into his arms, she decided that if she was ever going to be bold, now was the time. She had longed to brush the lock of hair over his forehead so many times. Without hesitating, she did it now. "Thanks for helping me tonight."

"I don't need thanks."

Was he saying he didn't want her? Or was he saying he didn't want sex to be a payback? "Why did you stay away so much this week?" she whispered.

"Joining our lives together isn't simple, Anita. I needed time to think. I thought you might, too."

"Are you having regrets?" she asked, needing to know the truth.

Slow to answer, he finally admitted, "Marriage isn't what I thought it would be."

"So you *do* have regrets." Her voice shook as her hands dropped away from him, and she began to move away.

With one quick motion, he wrapped his arm around her and pulled her close again. "No regrets. As I said, I'm just sorting things out. The truth is, I've never lived with anybody before. Not since I left home. It all takes some getting used to."

Her breasts against his chest, his arousal pressing against her most secret place, she almost moaned, "Tate, I'm not always sure what you want."

"Right now, I want you."

When his thumb tenderly trailed down her cheek and neck, her breath caught. But she knew she couldn't just enjoy; she had to give. As she stroked her hand down his broad back, he shuddered. Then he was kissing her and caressing her. Everything happened so fast that talking wasn't as important as what they were doing. Tate only broke their kiss to give her more pleasure—to caress her breasts and taunt her nipple with his tongue until she reached for him and made him groan.

As he rolled her onto her back and slid inside her, he commanded, "Wrap your legs around me."

When she did, he went deeper and she felt as if her whole world was Tate and the pleasure he could give her.

While he brought her with him to the edge of erotic sensation, she knew she wanted so much more than pleasure—she wanted Tate's love. Her climax echoed in his cries of completion. As he held her, for those few moments she felt as if they were truly one.

But then the day caught up with her. Thoughts of asking her husband about a woman named Donna fled in her need for sleep. The last thing she remembered was Tate's strong arm around her and his lips nuzzling her ear.

In the morning, she found a note on the pillow next to her.

Anita,
I didn't want to wake you. You could have another rough day with Marie. If you need anything while I'm gone, call Garth and Sandy. I'll be in meetings for the next day or so and don't know when I'll get a chance to call. You have my cell number if there's an emergency.
Tate.

She wished he'd awakened her. She wished she could have kissed him goodbye. She wished...

Tate said he'd had things to sort out. What things?

She was going to miss him...because she loved him. She wanted him around twenty-four hours a day, seven days a week. But did he feel the same about her?

Although he liked her kids, what did he feel about her?

When he got home, she was going to find out once and for all.

That day, as the medicine took effect, Marie was practically back to her old sunny self. That night, Anita couldn't believe how much she missed Tate, and so did the boys.

"When is Tate coming back?" Corey asked.

"I don't know for sure."

"If he comes back after we're in bed, will he wake us?"

Anita laughed. "He might think you need your sleep."

"What's he doin' in Dallas?" Jared asked as his fingers fumbled with the buttons on his pajama top.

The ironic thing was, she didn't exactly know. "He said he had meetings."

"About what?"

"I'm not sure."

"He's probably going to build houses there, too," Jared said as if that was the only conclusion anyone could come to.

"Maybe that's what he's going to do," Anita mused. "We'll ask him when he comes home."

The next day, with Marie's fever gone now, Anita took her to stay with Inez for a few hours while she ran errands and prepared for Tate's return. She would fry chicken tonight for the boys so there would be leftovers. This afternoon, she would make apple-raisin pie again because Tate liked it so much. At the meat counter in the grocery store, Anita chose two thick steaks. Tate had given her a generous food allowance, and now she not only bought the steaks, but two bunches of fresh cut flowers and a candle she could light in the bedroom. She wanted him to know she was glad to have him home again.

As she pulled a carton of milk from the refrigerated case, a male voice said, "Well, look who's here. If it isn't Mrs. Tate Pardell."

Unfortunately, Anita knew that voice. Pasting on a

polite smile, she lowered the carton of milk into her basket. "Hello, Kip. Did you have a day off work?" It was around noon and she couldn't imagine why he'd be grocery shopping now.

Waving a hand at his basket, he explained, "Just stopped in over my lunch break. I needed some chocolate milk and chips to go with my sub."

He looked at her basket—the steaks, the flowers, the candle and the milk. "I guess congratulations are in order. You sure are movin' up in the world."

There was no point talking to this man or trying to be polite. She put her hands on her cart and attempted to push away, but he caught the edge of her basket.

"No wonder you never wanted to consider going out with *me*. That's a shame because I'm moving up, too. I got a better job in Tyler with an outfit bigger than Pardell's. You could come visit me now and then."

The gall of the man infuriated her. "I doubt if you can understand the concept of fidelity, but as before when you propositioned me, I'm married. Vows are sacred to me."

Angry at his leering demeanor, she added, "Even if I weren't married, I would never consider going out with you. You're not the kind of man I would date."

His expression turned hard and angry. "I guess not. My bank account can't compare to Pardell's."

When she tried to push away again, he still held her cart steady. "I guess the truth is hard to face."

"You wouldn't know the truth if it bit you. Tate's bank account has nothing to do with me marrying him."

"Tell that to someone who doesn't know you as well as I do."

"You don't know me at all!"

"I heard enough from Larry. You thought you were better than he was, going to those night classes and all…drawing on your computer…thinking you were going to start some kind of business."

"I *have* started a business," she said quietly. "I have real goals and ambition, something Larry didn't know anything about."

"You always were Miss High-and-Mighty. Even when you didn't have two pennies to rub together. Now, maybe you wouldn't be so high-and-mighty if you knew exactly what Tate was doing in Dallas."

A chill ran down Anita's spine. "He has meetings in Dallas."

"Oh, he has meetings, all right. Donna's living in Dallas now."

That name made Anita's chills spread through her whole body.

"You do know about Donna, don't you?" he asked with a smug smile.

Still, she kept silent.

"She and Tate were engaged. Then she got a job in Dallas and, for some reason, the wedding got called off. I never did understand it. But you know how men like to revisit their past sometimes. I imagine that's what Tate's doing while he's there."

Anita had no idea whether Kip was feeding her truth or lies, and that was the whole problem.

This time, when she pushed at her cart, Kip didn't stop her, yet she felt his gaze on her back as she walked away.

After Anita picked up Marie, she went home, put the

groceries away and poured juice for her daughter. She was trying not to think, not to worry, not to feel. But she couldn't forget the inscription on the money clip.

All My Love, Donna

Tate wouldn't have kept the money clip if it hadn't been important, if that woman hadn't meant something to him.

All too vividly, she remembered her marriage to Larry—the credit card statements, the shame and humiliation knowing she wasn't enough for her husband, that he had turned elsewhere for physical satisfaction. Why wouldn't Tate do the same? If he and this Donna had had something strong... If he and Donna had had really good sex...

When Anita made love with Tate, she found the experience more than she'd ever dreamed. But did he? What kind of satisfaction did he find? What did he feel?

She didn't know.

It wasn't as if they were normal newlyweds. It wasn't as if they were making love every day. Maybe Tate had worked those long hours last week not to sort things out but because she wasn't what he expected...she wasn't what he'd hoped.

At midnight, Tate let himself into the house. He could have waited until tomorrow morning to drive home, but he'd wanted to get back tonight. He couldn't believe how much he missed his new family, how he missed coming home to the kids' squabbles and laughter, Marie's babbling, Anita's pretty face. The trouble was, the missing made him feel raw and vulnerable.

What was it about being with Anita that turned him inside out? What was it about making love to her that afterward he felt he needed concrete walls around him to protect himself?

He could have phoned Anita to tell her he was coming home tonight, but he hadn't been sure until he'd gone back to the motel room after his meetings, felt its desolate air and knew he couldn't wait a minute longer to get back home. On the road, he'd thought about calling her again, but it had been late. He hadn't wanted to wake her if she'd gone to bed.

Or was it that you just didn't know what to say? a voice inside him whispered. *Maybe you're just afraid to tell her how much you missed her. If you tell her, she'll have some power over you.*

The truth was, he didn't like the idea of *needing* anyone. He didn't like the idea that he was so attached to someone that if she left, the ache would never go away.

When he entered the bedroom, the bed was empty. Then he saw her, standing beside the dresser, not looking happy to see him.

"I thought you'd be in bed," he said roughly.

"I was. But when I heard the garage door, I got up. We need to talk."

"Is it the kids? Has something happened?"

"No, nothing's happened to the kids." Her hands went to the belt on her robe and she tightened it. "It's us. I need to know where you were."

"You know where I was. I was in Dallas."

After a long look at him, she asked stoically, "Did you have a meeting with Donna? We may not have a perfect marriage, but I won't stand by while you sleep with other women."

Donna's name on Anita's lips seemed incongruous somehow. "Donna? What do you know about Donna?"

"That's the problem. I don't know *anything* about Donna. Or *you* and Donna. I heard you were engaged. And I don't know what you are to each other now."

"We were engaged once. Who's been talking to you about her?" he asked tersely.

Anita's cheeks were spotted red with her emotion, and her eyes were wide with questions. He suddenly felt as if he were on the witness stand and the judge had brought down a verdict without even hearing his testimony.

"Kip Fargo ran into me at the grocery store. And he seemed more than willing to tell me about your lover."

"Fargo?" Everyone on Tate's crew had known about Donna and seen her ring. They'd heard his plans for the future and dreams about having kids. No one knew the truth of why the engagement had been broken. He hadn't wanted to look like a fool. No one except Garth and Sandy, that was. They had helped him get over it…get over a dream that had blown up before it could begin.

"Why in the hell would you listen to Kip Fargo?" he demanded angrily.

"I listened because *you* never told me about her."

In turmoil over a marriage that was changing his life and giving him feelings he'd never had before, pride rose up hard and fast with Tate's anger. "I don't know what Kip Fargo told you about Donna. Yes, she lives in Dallas. At least, last I heard. But I haven't seen her since we broke off our engagement. I can't understand why you'd make a judgment without even talking to me."

When he looked into her eyes, he knew why. "I am *not* anything like your former husband, Anita. If you can't trust me to keep my vows, then we don't *have* a marriage." He had to get away from the doubts in her eyes, from a past that had bitten both of them too deeply to heal. "I think maybe I'll go to my office in town and sleep there tonight."

"Tate—"

Everything he was feeling was simply too much to handle and too much to talk about. He didn't want to say something he'd regret.

Before he did, he left.

When Tate picked up the phone the next morning in his office, he was in a lousy mood. Beard stubble brushed his hand as he put the phone to his ear. "Pardell here," he barked.

"Tate, it's Anita."

He was still riled up, still more angry and unnerved than he wanted to be. "We can't discuss this over the phone. When I get home tonight—"

"I'm not calling about us. Ruth called and she was beside herself. Warren had a heart attack and she's at the hospital all alone. They don't have any family nearby and I feel as if…I feel as if I should be there with them. I'm going to take the kids and drive to Houston."

His heartbeat was very loud in his ears as he asked, "When are you leaving?"

"As soon as I get packed. She said the doctors won't

tell her anything, and the hospital is so big she can hardly remember where Warren's room is. I feel I need to do this."

Without thinking twice, he asked, "Do you want to leave the kids here with me?"

There were a few beats of silence. "No, I'm going to take them along. I'm not sure what I'll do when I get there, but in the long run, it might help Ruth to have them there."

Thinking about packing for the three kids and making the long drive by herself, he asked, "How are you going to handle all of this on your own?"

After a brief hesitation, she answered softly, "I handled my life on my own before I met you." Her voice became painfully sad. "I'm sorry I had doubts about you, Tate. I doubted you because I have no idea where you stand and how you really feel about me and our marriage."

She was giving him an opening...*if* he wanted it. The problem was, he didn't know what to say. Last night, when he'd gotten to the office, he'd been exhausted. He'd stretched out on the couch and fallen into a deep sleep, only realizing that something was still wrong when he was ready to bite a bear this morning when he'd awakened at first light.

"I don't know what you want me to say, Anita. We got married to protect your kids and build a family. With that has to come some trust."

"Are you saying you trust *me*?"

Her question rattled him almost as much as the idea that she was leaving. "As I said, we can't discuss this over the phone. If you feel you need to go to Houston, go. We'll work this out when you get back."

Silent moments ticked by until she responded, "All right." But her voice cracked on the second word. Then suddenly, she was composed again. "After I know something, I'll call you and tell you how Warren is."

"Thanks. I'd be grateful for that."

Anita said goodbye and hung up and Tate felt lower than he'd ever felt in his life.

Going through the motions for the rest of the day, Tate was mad as hell one minute, filled with energy that wouldn't let him quit the next. In the afternoon, he went out on one of the construction sites and walked the property. He still found no peace.

When he went home, he took care of the horses, but he didn't eat or sleep. After he stopped at a fast-food restaurant, he went back to his office, stared at the burger awhile and then tossed it away. The second night on his couch didn't deliver any more peace than the first.

The next day, Anita still didn't call, and he wasn't surprised. Sure, when she did, she'd tell him Warren's condition. But what else would she tell him? That she was going to stay in Houston and live with the Suttons?

That flash of brilliant insight left him in an even worse mood and he told himself all he needed was a good night's sleep in his own bed. Why he thought sleeping at the office would help anything was beyond him. He'd slept alone before Anita. He could sleep alone now.

But the night alone in his own bed felt like an eternity.

The following morning, he showered and dressed.

When he picked up his cell phone on the dresser, he saw there was a text message from Anita. Damn. When had it come in? She must have used Ruth's cell phone.

Clicking on the message function, he saw Warren is stable. Will call when I know more. Anita.

Obviously, she didn't want to talk to him.

Hooking his phone on his belt, he was about to pick up his wallet when he spotted the money clip lying there, holding his bills. The inscription was easy to read.

All My Love, Donna.

He'd kept the damn thing as a reminder that he'd been a fool, as a reminder to be cautious, as a reminder to let his head do the choosing, not another part of his body.

All of a sudden, he realized that the part of his body that had chosen Anita had been his *heart*. Had she seen this money clip on the dresser? What had she thought?

They had started out all wrong…and all right. He realized now that he had deep, abiding feelings for this woman who had become his wife. He had feelings that wrapped around him so tight he'd been afraid they'd strangle him. But they wouldn't. Those feelings were precious because they came from the best part of him, and he'd lacked the courage to share them with her. No wonder she had doubts. No wonder she'd let Kip Fargo get under her skin.

He remembered the night he'd told Anita how Jeremy had died. He'd felt naked. He'd thought it was enough. She'd understood everything he'd said. She'd helped him understand he had to let go of the guilt.

Now, he understood it wasn't enough to share a bit or a piece here or there. He had to share everything in his heart and soul with her. Then maybe she'd understand how deeply he felt about her, how deeply he loved her. He missed her and the kids desperately, and he wasn't going to miss them another day. He wasn't going to let another day go by without making his marriage to Anita what it should be. *If* it wasn't too late. *If* he hadn't ruined everything by being an arrogant, stubborn, prideful male.

His foot hard on the accelerator, he made the drive to Houston in record time. With his SUV in the hospital's parking garage, he set out to find Warren Sutton and his wife. Anita might not be here. She might be somewhere with the kids. But he had to start someplace. If he'd had any brains, he would have gotten her a cell phone when she'd moved in. Then *he* could have called *her.*

Still, what he had to say, he had to say in person.

The information desk directed him to the ICU on the fourth floor. The woman had explained there was a lounge up there where visitors waited until they could have their short visits with members of their family. To Tate's surprise, Ruth and Anita were sitting in the lounge, talking. Marie was on Ruth's lap while the boys sat coloring on the floor near Anita.

As soon as Anita saw him, her eyes widened and her mouth dropped open. Recovering, she asked, "What are *you* doing here?"

So this wasn't going to be as easy as he'd thought. "We belong together, not apart." He looked at the children. "I didn't think they'd allow kids in here."

"I just stopped here to see Ruth before—"

Ruth cut in. "Hello, Tate. Good to see you."

"How's Warren?"

"On the mend, we hope. He's going to have to change his diet drastically and get a membership at a health club. If he does those things, I might have him around another twenty years."

As her eyes filled with tears, she transferred Marie from her lap to her shoulder. "Boys, why don't you come with me? Let's take a walk. We'll go throw some pennies in the fountain in the courtyard."

Avoiding Tate's gaze, Anita fished pennies out of her wallet, handed a few to each boy and gave a weak smile to Ruth as she led the twins down the corridor.

When he turned to his wife, Tate took Anita's hands and tugged her up. "I don't want to do this here," he admitted, "but I don't want to wait another minute, either, so here goes. It's true Donna and I were engaged. But she didn't want *me*, she wanted my money. A week before we were supposed to be married, she used my credit cards to go on a spending spree like you've never seen. Not many people knew about that because I felt foolish that I hadn't seen through her. But I hadn't. So when you and I hooked up, I tried to be careful. The thing was, I never counted on falling for you so hard...or loving you so much. I've never loved any woman the way I love you, Anita."

As her lips parted in surprise, he rushed on. "I know your husband did you wrong. I know it might take time for you to see I'm not like him. But we've got time. The vows I made to you mean everything to me. Not only because we made a deal, but because I'm head over heart in love with you. Can you believe that?"

While Anita gazed into his eyes, hers filled with tears. "I can't believe you're saying these things. I can't believe you love me. I've dreamed about you loving me. Because *I* love *you*. I'm not sure how or when it happened, but it sure happened fast. And it scared me so badly, I've kept it to myself."

"Because you didn't know what I felt," he murmured, understanding completely.

She nodded. "When we made love, it was wonderful. But afterward, you turned away."

Pulling her closer so his breath touched her lips, he said in a low voice, "I turned away because I didn't have the courage to face what was happening between us. I didn't have the courage to hand you my heart and soul. But now I do. Can you believe I'll be faithful to you?"

Tenderly, she stroked her hand down his jaw and he knew everything was going to be all right.

"I know you're an honest man and will keep your vows," she returned with certainty. "I'm head over heart in love with you, too, Tate Pardell. I was on my way home to tell you that. I just stopped here to say goodbye to Ruth. I was going to come home and ask you if we couldn't come back down here together."

His arms went around her then, pulling her close, bringing their hearts together. His mouth on hers, he put everything he was feeling into his kiss. When she responded with the same wholehearted fervor, he knew he'd found his soul mate, and nothing on God's green earth could ever keep them apart again.

Epilogue

Tate's big dining room table was covered with a green cloth. Plates laden with every Thanksgiving delicacy imaginable sat in front of their guests and members of his family, including his own mom and dad.

Making sure everybody had exactly what they needed, Inez fluttered about. Upon discussion with his wife, Tate had decided to invite Inez to move into the housekeeper's quarters and be their built-in babysitter. It solved her dilemma of being alone in the world and gave Anita more time to work on her Web site business, as well as spend time with him—quality time.

"Only one helping of everything," Ruth Sutton warned her husband.

"I made a pumpkin pie suited for anyone on a diet," Anita told Warren with a grin. "No sugar and low fat."

"That's my kind of dessert," Sandy Finney said with a slow smile.

Her twins, as well as Corey and Jared, were seated at a small table of their own beside the big one, while Marie poked mashed potatoes into her mouth in her high chair.

Tate stood and clinked his spoon against his glass to capture everybody's attention. "This being Thanksgiving and all, I just wanted to say how grateful we are that all of you could make it." He gave his parents an extra-long look of gratitude, and they both smiled back.

Pulling Anita up beside him, he went on, "This year, I have exceptional blessings to give thanks for." With a nod to the small table, he listed those blessings by name. "Corey and Jared." He pointed to the high chair. "And precious Marie. Most of all, I'm giving special thanks this year for my wife. She's changed my heart and my life."

"Oh, Tate," he heard Anita murmur and saw the happiness well up in her eyes. He simply couldn't help himself. Before he could partake of the turkey and stuffing and pumpkin pie, he had to partake of her.

Bringing her close, unmindful of friends and family gathered around, he kissed her—a long, slow, sweet kiss that told her how glad he was that she was his wife. Ever since they'd returned from Houston, they couldn't seem to keep their hands off each other. Ever since they'd come back from Houston, he couldn't stop telling her how much he loved her and never tired of hearing the same words from her.

"Dad, can you cut the mushy stuff? The turkey's going to get cold," Jared complained.

A deep rumble began in Tate's chest and, when he broke the kiss, he could see Anita was laughing, too. Leaning close to her, he whispered in her ear, "We'll get to the *good*, mushy stuff later."

Reaching up, she brushed his hair over his brow and said, with heartfelt sincerity, "You make me feel like Cinderella."

"I'm more cowboy than Prince Charming."

"You're *my* Cowboy Prince Charming."

Hand in hand, they sat once more at the table, a table filled with a family Tate had missed for most of his life.

Squeezing Anita's hand, he sent up another prayer of thanks and then dug into the meal she'd prepared, intending full well to enjoy every minute of their happily-ever-after.

* * * * *

Watch for Karen Rose Smith's next book
from Silhouette Special Edition,
CUSTODY FOR TWO,
coming in May 2006.

SILHOUETTE *Romance*®

COMING NEXT MONTH

#1814 THAT OLD FEELING—Cara Colter
Accustomed to taking risks, Brandy King wants to bolt when her father asks her to help widower Clint McPherson through his emotional turmoil. Now this daredevil woman faces her greatest challenge—how to handle all the old feelings when she's reunited with this man who once broke her young heart….

#1815 SOMETHING'S GOTTA GIVE—Teresa Southwick
The weird phone calls and mysterious pop-up messages shook Jamie Gibson. But her new bodyguard has her definitely on edge. Sexy, dedicated Sam Brimstone has promised to keep her safe and then be gone. But trapped between the intense attraction she feels for Sam and the threat of an unknown stalker, Jamie knows that something's gotta give….

#1816 SISTER SWAP—Lilian Darcy
Can identical twins really swap places? Singer Roxanna Madison tries to adopt some of her sister's meeker characteristics for an important business trip to Italy. But her new boss, the gorgeous Gino di Bartelli, and his motherless child have her own heart and voice threatening to bubble to the surface.

#1817 MADE-TO-ORDER WIFE—Judith McWilliams
Billionaire Max Sheridan had assumed the etiquette expert he hired would be a dowdy grandmother. Instead, the beautifully dynamic Jessie Martinelli has his orderly mind turning from politeness to more, well, complicated matters of the heart. Is this expert about to give him a lesson in love?

SRCNM0406